The dog's squashy, square face was pressed against the front of the cage like he was trying desperately to see us. When he spotted me, his whole butt started wagging. He kept making these sweet whimper-yelp noises like, *Let me out! Please save me! I want to love you SO MUCH!*

"Oh, wow," I said, crouching so our eyes were level with each other. "Hello, dog."

"Ooooorrrrrrooo," he whimpered, squirming happily.

"He's pretty cool," Deandre said. "I mean . . . that'd be OK with me. If you like him."

"I don't just like him," I said. "I *love* him."

Get into some

Pet Trouble

Runaway Retriever

Loudest Beagle on the Block

Mud-Puddle Poodle

Bulldog Won't Budge

Oh No, Newf!

Smarty-Pants Sheltie

Bad to the Bone Boxer

Dachshund Disaster

Pet Trouble

Bad to the Bone Boxer

by T. T. SUTHERLAND

SCHOLASTIC INC.

New York   Toronto   London   Auckland
Sydney   Mexico City   New Delhi   Hong Kong

ISBN 978-0-545-20271-8 4430 0415
8/10

12 11 10 9 8 7 6 5 4 3 2 1   10 11 12 13 14 15/0

Printed in the U.S.A.   40
First printing, August 2010

For Naomi

CHAPTER 1

The truth is, I wanted to get a dog so my best friend would be my best friend again.

That plan didn't work out so well. In fact, it made things much, much worse.

But how was I supposed to know what would happen? Really, it was Mr. Sanchez's fault. He shouldn't have told me about the shopping trip.

It was a Saturday in October. I was done with all my homework, except for some stuff for Ms. Applebaum's big community service project, so Mom and Dad said it would be OK if I went over to my friend Rosie's to play with her new dog, Buttons.

But when I called the Sanchez house, Rosie's dad answered the phone and told me she wasn't there. Which would have been enough, right? That's all he had to say! "Sorry, Michelle, Rosie's not here. I'll tell her you called." And then my day would have been fine, and maybe the whole mess with Tombo never would have happened.

Instead, Mr. Sanchez said, "Sorry, Michelle, Rosie's not here. She's at the mall with her mom and Pippa."

Now why did he have to tell me that? I mean, really! Someone clearly has no understanding of the psychology of ten-year-old girls.

I said, "Thanks very much, Mr. Sanchez. Please let her know I called." And then I stood by the phone for five minutes, doing the deep breathing exercises Mom taught me to stop myself from crying. Of course, she also gave me a long speech at the same time about how crying is really OK and I should let my emotions out when I need to, but for instance, when you're in the middle of PE and your best friend just picked someone else for her team instead of you, *I* think that's maybe not the *best* time to "let out your emotions."

So I've gotten pretty good at the deep breathing exercises lately.

After a moment, my older brother popped his head over the banister of the stairs and stared at me.

"Uh," he said. "Michelle? I can hear you breathing from my room."

"So?" I said. "Would you like me to *stop* breathing? Is my *existence* bothering you, Deandre?"

His eyebrows shot up. "OK, I know *I* haven't done anything," he said. "So you must be projecting your anger at someone else onto me. Do you want to talk about it?"

This might be a good time to mention that our parents are both psychologists. They're really big on communication and family dynamics and talking through problems and all of that stuff. It has kind of rubbed off on me and Deandre.

"No," I said, sitting down on the bottom stair and resting my chin on my hands. The end of the bright green scarf tied around my hair slipped over my shoulder and I pushed it back. Not even the pretty dark green frogs printed on it could cheer me up.

Deandre sat down on the top step of the stairs. Our stairs go up to a landing, turn, go up to another landing, and turn again to go up to the top, so he was actually facing me, just one story up. He leaned against the wooden banister and waited.

Waiting is a trick he picked up from Mom. I guess it works on her patients all the time. If they say they don't want to talk, she just sits there calmly and quietly until they finally say something. She's had to wait more than one session sometimes. Not with me, though; the waiting trick can break me down in less than five minutes.

"All *right*," I said. "It's just Rosie."

"More Rosie trouble?" he said. "Haven't you guys been fighting for forever?"

"No, and we're not *fighting*," I said. "It's just this year. Fourth grade was so much easier than fifth grade." In fourth grade, Pippa was in a different class. In fourth grade, I was definitely Rosie's best friend. In fourth grade, she told me everything, and we were the ones who went on shopping trips together, and I never thought that she liked anyone else more than me.

But now Pippa was in Ms. Applebaum's class with us, and it was like Rosie spent every minute with her. Pippa went to her house nearly every day after school. Sometimes they invited me, too, but sometimes Rosie forgot — or, I was afraid, maybe sometimes she just decided she didn't want me there.

It's not that I mind Pippa. There's nothing *to* mind about Pippa; she's quiet and sweet and boring and practically not even there. It's not like she did this on purpose, I don't think. She doesn't seem clever or underhanded like that. But for some reason Rosie just *looooooves* her, and it makes everything all different from how it's supposed to be.

Deandre snorted. "You think fifth grade is hard?" he said. "Try —"

"— high school," I finished along with him. "Yeah, yeah, I know." He'd just started his freshman year and kept telling me horror stories about how big the high school was and how much work he had to do. He said it was better to prepare me so I wouldn't be surprised in four years, but I was like, *Um, that's OK, thanks anyway!*

"You should see how much geometry homework I have," he said, shaking his head.

"Hey, whose session is this, yours or mine?" I asked.

He grinned. Deandre decided to start wearing his hair in cornrows this year, which makes him look older and kind of cool. It almost makes me want to try something new with my hairstyle, although I've been pulling it back in one big curly puff since first grade and I love tying my different scarves around it, so I'm not sure I'm ready to change that yet.

"Maybe you just need to find something you and Rosie can connect over," Deandre said. "Something you have in common." He shrugged. "Or maybe you should get a new best friend. She's kind of loud anyway."

That's when I had my fantastic, terrible, brilliant, dreadful idea. I was so excited about it, I forgot to get mad at Deandre for insulting my best friend.

"That's it!" I said, jumping up. "You're so right!" I started to run off, then turned to wave back at him. "Thanks, Deandre!" Mom and Dad are also very big on expressing appreciation and saying "thank you" for everything.

"Uh-oh," I heard him mutter. "What —"

But I was already around the corner into Dad's office by then. He was sitting at his computer, writing one of his articles for some fancy psychology journal.

"DAD!" I shouted, and he jumped about three feet.

"Michelle!" he said, sounding shocked. "What have we discussed about polite interaction and inside voices?" He pushed his glasses up and gave me his stern look, which I happen to know he practices in the mirror sometimes, because I've caught him doing it. I've tried practicing a look like that, but nobody seems to take it seriously on me.

"Sorry," I said. "But I just had the *best* idea!"

My dad's office is actually a small room between the living room and the den, so through the door on the other side I could see my mom on the white leather couch, reading. She looked up from her book and I hurried around to the other side of Dad so they could both hear me.

"Ready?" I said. "I think we should get a dog!"

"A dog," my mom echoed, giving my dad an amused look.

"It would teach us responsibility," I said. "And we'd learn how to train it and take care of it and I bet you'd learn all kinds of cool things about the psychology of animals and maybe you could write some articles about that and dog psychology is totally a growing field right now so it would actually be really cool and —"

"Michelle, breathe," said my mom. But she was smiling.

"As it so happens," my dad said, "we've been thinking the same thing."

CHAPTER 2

We went straight out to the animal shelter that afternoon. I was so excited all the way there. I nearly pulled my scarf out of my hair four times because I was fidgeting with it so much.

This was going to change everything. Now I would have a dog and Rosie would have a dog and Pippa would just have her big, lazy cat. Rosie and I could take our dogs to the park together. She'd call me so our dogs could play with each other, and this time she'd forget to call Pippa instead. I'd have my best friend back.

Plus a dog! I didn't even care what kind we got. A dog is a dog, right? They run and play and lick your face and sleep on the couch while you watch TV. Easy and fun. That's what I figured.

If Dad had known what I was thinking, I bet I would have gotten an earful about unreasonable expectations and confronting reality. But I didn't need a lecture — because although I didn't know it yet, reality was going to confront me really hard in just a couple of hours.

"We're getting a dog!" I said, poking Deandre's shoulder.

"Ow," he said. "And yeah, I know. My ears do work, you realize."

"I had a corgi when I was your age, Michelle," Mom said to me. "Isolde — she was a sweetheart."

"We always had mutts," Dad said. "Loulou was the first purebred dog I ever owned."

Loulou was a retired racing greyhound Mom and Dad adopted soon after they got married. There are photos of me with her when I was two and Deandre was six, but I don't remember her. She was a really pretty dog, all long legs and a long elegant snout.

"Maybe we'll get another greyhound," Deandre said. I've seen photos of him and Loulou sleeping outside in the sun all curled up together like a pile of puppies.

"We'll see what's available," Mom said as we pulled into the Wags to Whiskers parking lot. "It'll probably be mostly mutts here, but that's OK. Your father and I think it's very important to adopt a dog from a shelter."

"So we can give it a good home!" I said. "Poor abandoned dog!" I loved the idea of saving a lonely dog and making it finally feel wanted.

The woman at the front desk was thrilled to meet us. Her name was Miss Hameed, and she had long dark hair coiled up in a thick bun on the back of her head. Her shirt was the same bright green as my hair scarf and she typed really, really fast.

She clapped her hands together as my parents talked to her. "Oh, we have some wonderful dogs here at the moment!" Her voice had a pretty accent where all the o's sounded more musical than usual. "I hope you find one that's right for you. We do our best to make them comfortable, but they could all use a great family to love them."

I grinned at Deandre. I was sure we would be a great family for any dog!

Miss Hameed led us through a door into a long concrete hallway. On either side of us were big, roomy cages, each with only one dog inside plus a bowl of water, a couple of toys, and a giant pillow or dog bed in the corner. It was a lot nicer than the shelters in the sad commercials on TV. But it still wasn't as nice as living in a real home with a family to take care of them.

Most of the dogs rushed to the front of their cages when they heard us come in, and a lot of them started barking. I put my hands over my ears, although that made it hard to hear Miss Hameed as she told my parents about the dogs.

In the first cage on my left, a German shepherd was lying on his pillow in the back corner. He just blinked at us sadly, like he was too used to disappointment to have any hope anymore. It made my chest hurt looking at his mournful face.

"Maybe we should take him," I said, tugging on my dad's sleeve.

"Miss Hameed says he's quite old," Dad said sympathetically. "He wouldn't be able to play with you very much. But we'll keep him in mind — don't set your heart on the first dog you see, honey."

A scruffy terrier mix was leaping up and down in the next cage, yipping frantically. Her brown eyes were wild with excitement and tufts of blond-brown fur stuck out all around her face.

"Oh!" I said. "Look how cute she is! And she really wants to come out and play!"

Mom and Dad exchanged glances. "That one might be a bit *too* high-energy for us," Mom suggested.

The third cage held a rotund pit bull mix, who just stood at the door panting at us with her long pink tongue hanging out. Her short fur was a pale whitish-blond with patches of dark brown, and her tail started to wag slowly when she saw us.

"Aww, she looks like she's smiling," I said, smiling back at her. She wagged her tail even more.

"Her owners gave her up because she wasn't aggressive enough," Miss Hameed said. "Can you imagine? Poor girl. She's a big teddy bear, but nobody wants her because she looks like a pit bull, and they have a terrible reputation."

"*I* want her!" I said.

Dad laughed. "We can't take *all* of them, Michelle."

"She's on a very strict diet right now," Miss Hameed said. "She's dangerously overweight because her owners never exercised her and they let her eat whatever she wanted." She started telling my parents about the diet, but I stopped listening because I saw the dog in the next cage.

He was up on his hind legs with his front paws hooked on the wire mesh. His squashy, square face was pressed against the front of the cage like he was trying desperately to see us. When he spotted me, his whole butt started wagging so hard he knocked himself to all fours, and then he started bouncing his front paws up and down on the floor. He kept making these sweet whimper-yelp noises like, *Let me out! Please save me! I want to love you SO MUCH!*

"Oh, wow," I said, crouching so our eyes were level with each other. "Hello, dog."

"Ooooorrrrrrrooo," he whimpered, squirming happily.

"That's a boxer," Deandre said from behind me.

"I know," I said, although I'd only been guessing. He was a warm brown color all over except for a swath of white down his chest and a little stripe of white between his eyes. He had long, slender legs and a sturdy solid body with really short fur. His ears were floppy and his nose was a bit squashed and he had the most enormous sweet brown eyes. There were adorable wrinkles on his forehead, as if he was *tremendously* worried that I wouldn't like him.

He wasn't small and fluffy like Rosie's dog. He was practically ten times the size of her poodle puppy, Buttons. But I'd seen Buttons with other dogs; she had no idea how small she was, and I was sure she would play with anyone.

Plus, this dog's whole face radiated how much he

wanted to be loved. I was good at loving things. I was sure I could make him happy.

Behind him in the cage was a strange mess. Bits of white fluff were scattered from one wall to the other next to the remains of disemboweled toys. His dog bed looked like it had been nibbled around the edges. His metal water bowl was upside down in a puddle in the middle of the floor.

Of course, I didn't recognize the warning signs at the time. I didn't even think about them until later. All I noticed right then were the dog's big, hopeful brown eyes.

"He's pretty cool," Deandre said. "I mean . . . that'd be OK with me. If you like him."

The boxer pressed his face against the mesh again, gazing out at me. *Please please please please PLEASE love me*, said his eyes.

"I don't just like him," I said. "I *love* him."

The dog's butt started wagging frantically again, as if he'd understood me. I knew my parents would want me to look at all the other dogs in the shelter before I made up my mind. But it wouldn't make any difference.

I'd found my dog.

CHAPTER 3

I wished we could have taken all the shelter dogs home. There were so many sad, hopeful faces in there. But Mom and Dad loved the boxer, too, and Miss Hameed said he needed a home where people would play with him a lot and exercise him every day. That sounded like us to me! We love to go hiking and we have a huge backyard for running around in. Plus, I was already planning the playdates with Buttons in my head.

"He's less than a year old," Miss Hameed said, opening the cage door and clipping a leash onto the dog's collar. "His first family got him as a puppy, but they didn't realize how big he would get. They left him here a few weeks ago . . . they said they just couldn't handle him anymore, especially since they're about to have a new baby."

"That's so sad," I said. I held out my hand so the boxer could sniff it. He immediately dragged his huge pink tongue over my fingers and I giggled, which made his butt wag happily again.

"They called him Ali," Miss Hameed said. "Get it? Because he's a boxer?"

Deandre laughed. "Sure," he said. "He doesn't look much like Muhammad Ali to me, though."

"You can change his name," Miss Hameed said with a smile.

"Can we call him Tombo?" I asked Mom and Dad. "Like the boy in *Kiki's Delivery Service*?" That's one of my favorite movies. I love Japanese cartoons and anime, especially all the movies by the director Miyazaki like *Spirited Away* and *Castle in the Sky* and *Ponyo*. I like how they feel like dreams and there are all these weird creatures in them and they're funny and surprising.

Rosie doesn't get those movies at all — she says they're too slow and too weird and that we're too old for cartoons, which is silly because even grown-ups like those movies and they're much cooler than the cartoons you see on TV.

"I looked it up once," I said to Deandre. " 'Tombo' means 'dragonfly' in Japanese."

Deandre pointed at the big brown wriggly dog. "He doesn't look much like a dragonfly either!"

"I kind of like it," Mom said. "Tombo. It's cute."

Dad nodded, and Deandre shrugged. "Sure," he said. "It's fine with me. Hey, Tombo!"

The dog immediately whipped his head around to look at Deandre. His ears flopped forward and his whole wrinkly face went alert, making his jowls wobble.

"He likes it!" I said, grinning. "Good boy, Tombo!" I scratched behind his ears and he lurched closer to me, bumping his heavy torso into my knees. He felt totally different from Buttons. She's small and floppy and light, like a cotton ball. Tombo was solid all the way through, like a bowling ball. I rubbed his shoulder and felt the strong muscles rippling in his chest and back.

After Mom and Dad finished the paperwork stuff with Miss Hameed, we all piled in the car and drove to Furry Tails, the pet store a few blocks over. She'd loaned us a leash and collar, but we needed to buy all the other important dog stuff we needed.

I realized we were lucky to have a pretty big car — Tombo took up more space in the backseat than Deandre did! He sat in between us, swiveling his head around at every noise and trying to lunge over me to the window whenever he thought he saw something interesting outside.

"OOOF!" I yelped as his full weight hit my legs. "Tombo, what are you being crazy about? Down! Or off! Or something!"

Deandre hooked his fingers into Tombo's collar and dragged him back to the middle of the seat. Tombo flopped down with his back legs stretching over Deandre's lap and rested his chin on my thigh, panting. I stroked the smooth fur between the wrinkles on his forehead, and he rolled his big brown eyes up to gaze at me. It was like he was saying, *Do you mean it? You're going to keep me? Are you sure? This is for real?*

"I think Tombo might have some insecurity issues," I said. "He just wants to be liked, but he worries that nobody really likes him the way he is."

"Awww," Dad said from the front seat.

"We like you, Tombo," Deandre said. "Of course, we've only known you for five minutes. I guess you could still change our minds."

"Deandre!" I said, covering Tombo's ears. "Don't even say such a thing!"

"We're here!" Mom said, pulling into a spot in front of Furry Tails. Tombo lunged to his paws again and nearly catapulted himself through the windshield. He was wriggling all over with excitement and, I think, nervousness.

"It's OK, shhh, calm down," I said, yanking on Tombo's leash. "Tombo! *Calm down!*"

"Maybe we should leave him in the car," Mom suggested.

"Can't we take him inside?" I pleaded. "I'll hang on to him and he'll be good, I promise."

That was my first lesson in not making promises about Tombo's behavior.

He stayed beside me as we walked up to the door, but as soon as we stepped inside the pet store, his ears perked up and he tried to bolt toward the toy aisle. I was dragged halfway across Furry Tails before I managed to throw all my weight backward and stop him in his tracks. He pawed at the air a few times and then turned to look at me with a baffled *Why are you thwarting me?* expression.

"I'll go get a crate and a bed," Dad said, patting my shoulder.

"I'll handle food and dog dishes," Mom said.

"We'll get a leash and some toys," Deandre suggested.

"Just get two toys to start with," Dad said. "We'll see what he likes."

Tombo's tongue flopped out and his butt started to wag again. His eyes were like, *Toys? TOYS? Did someone say TOOOOOYYYYYS?*

"You want me to take his leash?" Deandre offered.

"No, I got it, thanks," I said, wrapping the end more firmly around my hand. Sure, Tombo weighed as much as I did, but I was determined to learn how to manage him. Otherwise I'd never get to walk him or take him to the park by myself, and that would defeat the whole purpose of having my own dog!

Deandre and I headed for the toy section in a stop-and-go jerky way. Tombo would lunge forward, and then I'd drag him back, and then we'd take two steps and he'd lunge forward again. My hand was starting to hurt from the tightness of the leash around it. I gritted my teeth and planted my feet, forcing him to go at our pace, but it was a relief when we reached the aisle and he started sniffing all the toys in his cute, ridiculously overjoyed way.

My relief didn't last long. Half a minute later, Tombo snagged a giant stuffed duck between his jaws and yanked it off the display, sending a whole cascade of stuffed toys tumbling onto the floor.

"Ack!" I yelled. "Tombo, no! Drop it!"

He shook his head vigorously and the duck went *QUAAAAAAAAACK QUAACK QUAACK!* Tufts of bright yellow fur flew out in all directions.

Deandre started grabbing toys and sticking them back on their hooks. "Uh, I think we might be stuck with that one," he said.

QUAAAAAAACK! Tombo and the duck agreed. His teeth firmly gripped the toy and he was not letting go. No matter how hard I tried to pry the duck out of his mouth, it wasn't moving. So I put my hands on my hips and tried to give the dog a stern face instead, but he looked so funny with this huge fat yellow duck stuffed into his mouth that I started laughing.

"My dog loved that toy too," said a voice behind me.

I turned around and saw Midori Takashi, from my class at school. Her twin brother, Satoshi, was at the other end of the aisle, rolling a giant green ball between his hands as if he was checking on how sturdy it was.

Midori's straight black hair was pulled back into a ponytail and clipped with a plum-colored barrette. Her long-sleeved shirt was dark purple and she was wearing a gray hooded sweatshirt over it. Satoshi, on the other hand, was wearing a bright red sweater with orange flecks, as if they were deliberately trying to clash with each other as much as possible.

It was a little weird that Midori was talking to me. I mean, she's never been *un*friendly, but she mostly hangs out with her brother and his guy friends. Rosie always said Midori must be either a tomboy or boy-crazy, because she hardly ever talks to girls. She's also some kind of major genius who could have skipped, like, all of elementary school if she wanted to, but she decided to stay in the same grade with her brother instead. That was the rumor I'd heard, anyway.

"Well," Midori said, still talking about the duck, "I mean, she loved it until she totally destroyed it, which took about a day." She smiled and half-shrugged with one shoulder.

"Wow, really?" I said. "Well, I'm sure he won't do that."

Midori raised an eyebrow at my dog.

I glanced down at Tombo. He had the duck pinned under one paw and was ferociously trying to rip off one of the little flappy wings on the side.

"Hey, stop!" I said, reaching for the duck.

An explosion of white fluff burst out of the side of the toy and Tombo lurched back with the tiny wing poking out of his teeth. His eyes were wide and startled, like, *Whoa! What just happened? Did I win?*

"Yeah," Deandre said. "We definitely have to buy that toy now."

"Oh, Tombo!" I said. "What fun are toys if you're just going to ruin them right away?"

"Try this one," Midori said, pulling a blue woven rope toy off the hooks. "My dog can chew on these knots for ages, and it's survived a surprisingly long time."

"Thanks," I said. I gave it to Deandre so he could hold it out of Tombo's reach. I wanted to ask Midori more questions about her dog, but I couldn't help thinking about what Rosie would say if she saw us. If I was on a mission to get my best friend back, I probably shouldn't start by hanging out with a girl Rosie thought was so weird.

So instead I said, "Well, see you at school."

"Yup," Midori said, turning back to her brother. See? She didn't really want to talk to me either.

"She seems cool," Deandre said as we headed for the leash section. Tombo was desperately miserable about leaving all those other toys behind. I had to pretty much drag him along behind me. His nails scrabbled and squeaked against the tile floor and his head twisted around to look back at the toys with his sweet furrowed brow.

"I guess," I said. "I don't know her that well."

Someone in the next aisle dropped something on the floor with a clatter, and Tombo nearly leaped out of his skin. He bounced into the air and lunged sideways, flailing with alarm, and managed to knock over an entire display of leashes and collars.

"Tombo!" I yelped. "Man! Calm down!"

"Maybe you should wait outside with him," Deandre suggested, crouching to pick up the mess.

"Yeah, you're right." I wrapped Tombo's leash around my hand one more time and gave him a firm tug. "Come on, Tombo."

His head drooped as if he knew he was in trouble and he padded slowly beside me as we went out onto the sidewalk outside the store. The parking lot was half-full of cars, with people hurrying in and out of the stores and little puddles everywhere from when it had rained earlier in the morning. I knelt beside Tombo and rubbed my hand between his ears.

"It's all right," I said. "You didn't mean it. We just have to get used to each other. I know you want to be a good boy."

He poked his nose into my neck and slobbered a little. Then he noticed my scarf for the first time. I felt his teeth fasten on it as he tried to drag it loose from my hair.

"AAH! NO!" I shouted, ducking away from him. I grabbed the other end of my scarf and pulled. Tombo pulled back. With a horrible tearing sound, my pretty green scarf started to rip in half.

"Tombo, NO!" I yelled.

He dropped his end of the scarf, hunched his shoulders, and gave me a woeful, bewildered look, like, *What? Aren't we playing?*

"My poor scarf!" I said, sitting down on the concrete beside Tombo and holding the ruined fabric between my hands. The dark green frogs on his end were wet with slobber. "Oh, Tombo. What are we going to do with you?"

He leaned his massive weight against my side and rested his chin on my shoulder. His eyes said, *I'm sorry. I'll try to be good. I promise, I really will!*

Still, I was starting to worry. Tombo's last owners had given him up because they couldn't handle him anymore. I didn't want to give up on him like his first family had.

But what if he was too much for us to handle too?

CHAPTER 4

I felt better when Tombo fell asleep on my lap in the car on the way home. He nuzzled his heavy head against my jeans and made snorty, sleepy noises and it was really sweet. I told myself that we could help him. He was like one of Mom's or Dad's patients — we just had to understand him and then figure out how to make him better. It would be good practice for when I become a psychologist one day. Maybe if I was good at it, I would even decide to be an animal psychologist. That could be pretty cool!

Tombo bolted awake when the car stopped in our driveway. He stepped all over my lap again trying to see out the window. I was going to have serious dents in my thighs if this kept happening.

I held on to him tightly, but he still dragged me up the stairs from our garage to the front door. His paws bounced against the stone slabs of the front deck as he watched Mom get out her keys. His muscles rippled under his short brown fur.

"We should take him for a walk later," Dad suggested, patting Tombo's head. "Get some of this wild energy out."

"That would be great!" I said. "Maybe we can take him to the park, and maybe Rosie will be there with Buttons!"

Deandre narrowed his eyes at me, like he was starting to figure out my whole plan. But before he could say anything, Mom got the door open and Tombo bolted inside with me hanging on for dear life behind him.

Tombo barely stopped to explore. He just wanted to romp from room to room, whip his head around, sniff the air, and then charge into the next room. We went in a whole circle around the bottom floor and then thundered up the stairs so he could poke his nose into each bedroom.

The cute part, though, is that he totally figured out which room was mine. He nudged the door open with his nose, took one look around, and sauntered inside like he knew he belonged there. He lay down on my zebra-print rug and flopped onto his back, panting and grinning sideways at me.

I love having a room that says a lot about me, although I know it's more of a messy mishmash than Rosie's perfectly pink coordinated room. One reason I know this is because Rosie is always telling me so. Every time she comes over, she's like, "There are too many colors in this room! Nothing matches the way it should! This bookshelf could be so much neater. Oh, and you should really think about a shoe rack." She has offered to help me redecorate and organize it about a million times, but I keep putting her off because I really like it the way it is . . . although it's hard to tell her that!

A giant *Spirited Away* poster hangs on the wall, next to a big collage of photos from our last trip to Kenya to visit my grandparents. A circle of small framed photos of me hangs over the bed — me with elephants, me with giraffes, me with antelopes, and me with lions really far off in the distance behind me. My bedspread is a quilt made by my American grand-mother, using colors and scraps of fabric from my favorite scarves, so it's green and blue and orange and gold with hints of jungle leaves and ocean waves and herons and monkeys and lizards all over the place.

The wide white bookshelf has books about psy-chology shoved in next to manga novels, the Little

House series, *Monsoon Summer*, and *Coraline*. I have a plan to arrange them alphabetically by author one day, but I haven't had time yet. There's a corkboard over my desk which has a bunch of stuff pinned to it . . . I keep meaning to clear it off, but instead I just keep adding things. Like my second-place ribbon for the creative writing contest last year, and the photo-booth pictures of me and Rosie together at the carnival over the summer, and a napkin my cousin got signed for me by one of the voice actors from *Princess Mononoke*, and this really funny ad I tore out of a magazine with a close-up of a dog's face slurping his long tongue over his nose. He looked a bit like Tombo, actually, now that I noticed it.

My zebra-print rug is fuzzy and soft under my feet — I never wear shoes in my room — and it's big enough to stretch almost from one bright green wall to the other. I don't have a computer in my room, but I do have a phone that's shaped like a monkey holding a banana up over its head. I picked up the banana part and dialed Rosie's number. Surely she had to be back from the mall by now.

"Hello?" It was one of Rosie's brothers. She has four of them, so I never guess who's answered the phone, just in case I'm wrong, which would be embarrassing. I was pretty sure it wasn't Danny, though, because I think I'd recognize his voice.

"Hey, is Rosie there?" I asked. "It's Michelle."

"Sure," he said. "ROOOOOSIEEEEE!" he bellowed without covering the phone. I rubbed my ear, and Tombo lifted his head to peer at me like, *Is that you making all that noise?*

I could hear a lot of commotion on the other end of the phone, which is normal for Rosie's house. It always seems like there are at least fifteen people there, between her family and all their friends.

"Buttons, STOP!" Rosie shrieked. "Hello?"

"Hey!" I said. "Guess what!"

"Oh, hey Michelle," she said. "Hang on. *Buttons!* Tags are not for chewing on! Get out of that shopping bag! BUTTONS, COME BACK HERE WITH MY NEW SHIRT! Hang on, Michelle." The phone clattered out of her hand and I heard her hollering and chasing Buttons in the background. I wasn't one hundred percent sure, but I thought I could hear another girl's voice too. And it wasn't hard to guess who that might be.

"OK," Rosie said breathlessly into the phone. "Sorry. Buttons seems to think anything that comes in a bag must be a new toy for her. I'd better put away these sweaters before she attacks them." Rustling and crinkling noises from her end.

"Did you have fun at the mall?" I asked casually, so she'd know I knew she'd gone without me, even though I didn't really want to hear the answer.

"Yeah, totally!" Rosie said, like it was no big deal and she hadn't even thought of inviting me and it wouldn't ever occur to her that I might care. "Pippa and I found this way cool little store where everything was on sale and Mom let me get *three* new sweaters because they were so cute and cheap. Even Pippa got one! You wouldn't have liked them, though; everything was those pale pastel colors you hate."

"I don't hate them!" I said. Was Rosie making a point about how she wears pink and Pippa wears plain boring white and brown and blue while I always wear something bright and multicolored? Was she saying she didn't like my scarves? "I have plenty of pale-colored things."

"Oh, I didn't know that," Rosie said. "I just figured, since your scarves are so colorful. There was, like, nothing in this store that would match any of them."

I doubted that; I have scarves in every color you can imagine. I glanced at the coatrack in the corner of my room, where I hang all my scarves so I can see them, like a rainbow tree.

"Well, I couldn't have come with you anyway," I said. *Even if I had been invited. AHEM.* "Because guess what we did today?"

"What?" Rosie said. She started giggling before I could say anything. "Oh my gosh, Buttons is doing the cutest thing right now. She's, like, jumping all over Pippa trying to get to her face. Well, it was your fault for sitting down on the floor! That's totally asking for a face licking! Oh, Buttons, you silly thing."

"WE GOT A DOG," I said loudly, trying to keep her attention on me instead of Pippa and Buttons.

It worked. For a moment Rosie didn't say anything at all.

"A dog?" she said finally. "You did? Wait, a real dog?"

"Yeah, of course a real dog," I said. "He's so cute. I want you and Buttons to meet him!"

"Hmm," Rosie said. "Has he had all his shots? Buttons is still a puppy and she's only supposed to hang out with dogs that are —"

"Yes, of course he has," I interrupted her. "Maybe we could meet at the park? Dad said we might take a walk over there later."

Tombo surged to his paws at the word "walk" and blinked at me several times. When I stayed sitting on the bed, he shook himself from ears to tail with a funny flapping sound and then came over to rest his chin on the quilt beside me, giving me big mournful eyes.

"Maybe," Rosie said. "I'll check with my mom. Buttons already had kind of a busy day. Danny ran off with her, can you believe it? That's why Mom took us to the mall, because Danny took her to his friend Noah's house to practice her agility training which is *so* unfair because she's supposed to be *my* dog and *I'm* the one who should be training her and he didn't even invite me, can you believe it?"

I wanted to be like, "Wow, it sucks when you're not invited somewhere, doesn't it?" But I was afraid she'd get mad and it would turn into a fight and then Tombo and Buttons wouldn't get to meet until we'd spent at least a week not talking to each other.

So instead I said, "That is so lame. You must have been mad."

"I know, right?" Rosie said. "So he was there for, like, EVER and she was jumping over things and running around with Yeti and Merlin and Jeopardy and so I bet she's really tired, poor little puppy."

She didn't sound tired to me — not if she was jumping all over Pippa and stealing Rosie's new clothes to play with. Was there some reason Rosie didn't want to meet my new dog?

"OH and GUESS WHAT?!" Rosie suddenly shouted at the top of her lungs. I winced and held the banana a little farther from my ear, shaking my head at Tombo. Of course, she didn't wait for me to guess. "*Guess* who I saw at the mall? Coming out of the movie theater and going to the food court? *Eric Lee.*" She paused as if this was a big pronouncement.

I had to think for a minute to figure out who Eric Lee was. He's a sixth-grader, the quiet one who's friends with Rosie's brother Danny. Everyone says he's really good with computers, but I didn't know much about him, except that Rosie mentioned him sometimes.

"Oh?" I said. "That's, uh —"

"WITH A GIRL," Rosie announced. "Eric Lee WITH A GIRL. They were *holding hands.* Can you *believe* it?"

I couldn't, really, not from the little I knew of Eric, but I didn't see that it was anything all that exciting. Certainly not more important than talking about my new dog. Rosie hadn't even asked what his name was yet.

"It was that Rebekah Waters," Rosie said. "Her dog is really cute, but I knew she was trouble. She's, like, *too* nice."

Kind of like Pippa? I wanted to say. "Why do you care?" I asked instead.

"I don't!" she nearly shouted. "I don't care! I just thought it was interesting. Jeez, Michelle, why do you always ask so many questions? I mean, whatever, I was just *telling* you. Not because *I* care or anything. Anyway, I should go, like, take Buttons outside. She's totally about to figure out how to get to my new sweaters. Have I mentioned that she's a genius? She's been so great in her agility class, better than anyone else, except maybe that Sheltie, Jeopardy, but if you ask me Buttons is cuter. Uh-oh, she's pawing my leg. That means she really has to go, sorry."

"Oh, OK," I said. "So about the park . . . ?"

"Maybe tomorrow," she said. "I'll call you tomorrow, OK? Pippa, that looks *so* great on you! You should go back and get five more! 'Bye, Michelle!"

And then she hung up.

I lay back on my bed and did some more deep breathing exercises.

Tombo's front paws hit the bed with a thump and he leaned toward me, sniffing curiously.

"It's OK," I said. "She's just busy. We'll meet Buttons tomorrow, don't worry."

His butt wagged and his tongue lolled out as if he was saying *I'm not worried! Everything is great! I love it here! Thank you for loving me!*

I rolled over and wrapped my arms around his neck. He licked my ear, and for some weird reason that made me feel better.

"Well, we don't need Buttons," I said. "Let's go to the park anyway!"

CHAPTER 5

My hand still felt squeezed and sore from being yanked around at the end of the leash, so I let Deandre hold Tombo's leash on the way to the park. It made me feel better to see that my brother had just as much trouble as I did. It was like Tombo didn't know how to walk in a straight line. He kept lunging off in one direction or another, or stopping suddenly so we all bumped into him, or whirling around to bound back the way we'd come. Somehow we kept ending up with the leash wrapped around our feet.

"Boy, I hope this tires him out," Dad said. He looked a little worried.

On our way into the park, I saw a bunch of sixth-graders playing Frisbee on one of the big fields. I recognized Rosie's brother Danny and his friends Parker and Troy. Heidi Tyler and Rory were there, too, along with a guy I didn't know, but I'd seen him around school for the past week, so I guessed he was new.

Three dogs were flopped on the grass nearby, watching them play. The golden retriever was Merlin — everyone knew Merlin because he'd showed up at school twice in the first week. He'd followed Parker there because he didn't want to be separated from him. Isn't that the cutest thing ever? I loved Tombo already, but I wasn't entirely convinced that he'd be smart enough to do something like that.

An enormous shaggy black-and-white dog sprawled next to Merlin, fast asleep. And on his other side, a small, pretty Sheltie had her ears up alertly. Her black eyes were focused on the Frisbee like laser beams, and her fur fluffed out around her as her head whipped back and forth each time it flew by.

Dad saw where I was looking. "Do you want to go say hi?" he asked. "We could see how Tombo reacts to those dogs."

That idea made me nervous. What if Tombo was a total freak in front of all those sixth-graders? Especially Danny, who'd definitely go home and tell Rosie about it. I didn't want Rosie to hear about Tombo before she met him, because I was sure that

Buttons would love him if they just got a chance to meet.

Plus, I wouldn't admit this to anyone, but I kind of like Danny a little bit, maybe. He's like a boy version of all the things I like about Rosie — they're both funny, and they say what they're thinking, and they're not afraid of anything, and they have all these crazy ideas which they'll actually do instead of just talking about them. But I don't want Rosie to know that I maybe like her brother, because I think she'd be all weird about it. And if she found out I'd hung out with him without her, she might get suspicious.

"No, that's OK," I said. "Let's just take him to the dog run."

Deandre looked relieved. "Yeah, I need a break from the leash," he said, flexing his hand and stretching his shoulder.

There weren't any other dogs in the dog run, so we felt safe taking off Tombo's leash. He galloped around for a minute, sniffing the hedges and peeing about a million times (I guess to let other dogs know he'd been there). I loved his gawky, long-legged run; it made him look a little off-balance, like he was constantly surprised at how strong and fast he was.

Deandre pulled a tennis ball out of his pocket and

whistled. Tombo's head shot up and he blinked at us from the far side of the water fountain. His face was like, *Did you hear that? I swear I heard something! What was it? Where did it come from? Let's find it and stalk it and attack it and shake it and HEY WHAT'S THAT IN YOUR HAND?*

"Tombo, fetch!" Deandre called, flinging the tennis ball down the length of the dog run.

The boxer leaped into action, bounding after the ball in a brown blur. He caught up to it as it bounced under one of the benches on the far end. Tombo didn't stop; he flung himself to the ground and shoved his whole head under the bench, wriggling and wagging his rear end.

"Good boy, Tombo!" I called. "Now bring it back! Bring the ball!"

Tombo backed out and turned to look at us. The tennis ball was bright green between his teeth, giving him a goofy half-open kind of Frankenstein grin.

Deandre whistled again. "Come on, Tombo!" My dad clapped his hands and crouched, waving at Tombo encouragingly.

Slowly and deliberately, Tombo set his butt on the ground, then carefully lay down, pinned the ball between his teeth, and started to chew.

"No!" I yelled. "Tombo! No chewing!"

We ran across the dog run to him, but by the time we got there, it was already too late. Tombo had crunched the tennis ball right in half, leaving a long strip of green peeling off to one side and a tragic mauled ball carcass covered in teeth marks. He shook it triumphantly as we hurried up to him and deposited it at my feet with a flourish.

"Holy — that is — I can't even —" Deandre sputtered.

"Tombo," I said, putting my hands on my hips. "You wicked dog! You were supposed to play with that, not destroy it!" Tombo wagged his butt and beamed at me. How was I supposed to yell at him when he kept giving me such a sweet, confused face?

"How did he do that so fast?" Dad said.

"Crazy teeth and destructo-powers," I said.

"He's working out his aggression issues," Deandre suggested. "Like that case you were studying last month, Dad."

"He's not aggressive!" I said. "He's sweet. He just thought we'd given him something to chew up. He didn't know he wasn't supposed to."

"But why would you do that to a tennis ball?" Deandre wondered. He picked up the remains gingerly between his fingers and carried it over to the trash can.

Dad rubbed his bald head, looking even more worried. "Whatever his reasons," he said, "let's just hope he doesn't do it to anything else."

CHAPTER 6

The only good news was that the walk and playing at the park did seem to tire out Tombo. He conked out on top of my feet while we all watched a movie after dinner, and later, when I showed him the dog bed set up next to mine, he got into it and rested his chin on the fluffy edge, watching me until I got into bed and turned off the light. A few minutes later, I heard him snoring softly.

"Good night, Tombo," I whispered. "Tomorrow will be much better, I'm sure."

That would probably have been another good moment for one of Dad's lectures about unreasonable expectations.

I woke up early on Sunday morning — *really* early. Through my forest-green curtains I could see that the sky was still that kind of in-between gray before the sun is really up. Clouds were whisking quickly across the sky, as if a storm was coming, and flurries of orange and gold leaves swirled past the window.

I yawned and stretched. Why was I awake this early? Had something woken me?

Crunch crunch crunch.

I froze. Uh-oh.

Throwing the covers back, I sat up and turned on the lamp beside my bed.

Tombo looked up with a startled expression. He was sprawled out in the middle of the rug with his back legs flopped to either side, busily chewing on something black and shiny. He blinked for a moment, and then his eyes met mine and his long pink tongue unfurled from his mouth. He panted at me in a cheerful, *Well it's about TIME you woke up!* kind of way.

"Tombo, what do you have?" I groaned. He planted one big brown paw over his treasure, as if daring me to come get it.

I rolled out of the bed and knelt in front of him. It was worse than I'd thought.

I mean, I'd guessed it was a shoe from the shape of it and the laces dangling off the sides. But it wasn't just any shoe — it was one of my *dad's* shoes. The fancy black leather pair he wore to his office for meetings with patients or other doctors. The pair he shined and polished carefully twice a week. They usually sat neatly on the shoe rack inside the front door, next to Mom's low black heels and my orange Converses and Deandre's white sneakers and my green flip-flops. How had one of them gotten up *here*?

Not that it was too hard to guess. I'd left my bedroom door open a crack in case Tombo wanted to go downstairs in the night and find his dog food. We'd left kibble out in his dish, since he hadn't wanted to eat anything all day.

"Tombo!" I whispered. "This is not what you were supposed to eat! Shoes, yuck! Gross! And you'll be in big trouble!"

I reached for the shoe and Tombo seized it in his jaws. I could see tooth marks all over the smooth black leather, and the laces were nibbled to shreds. Tombo's eyes darted from my face to my hand, as if he was waiting for me to try and wrestle the shoe away.

Well, I did try. I grabbed the heel end and tugged. I tried to yank it loose. I swung it up and down to see if I could lever the shoe out of his mouth. I leaned back and pulled as hard as I could, but Tombo dug his paws in and tried to back away, making small growling, grunting noises. His tiny stub of a tail was going nuts, so I knew he thought we were playing. But it wasn't a very fun game for me. I kept picturing Dad's face when he woke up and saw what had happened to his shoe.

Suddenly Tombo gave a fierce yank, and I lost my grip on the shoe and fell over backward with a thump. He stepped back, then toward me, wagging his butt and looking tremendously pleased with himself. His face was like, *Awesome! Again, again!*

"I don't *want* to play tug-of-war with you!" I snapped. "Tombo, give it to me!"

Maybe he could finally hear the grumpiness in my voice, because his butt slowly stopped wagging, and then his head drooped, and he gently set the shoe down on the floor. His soft brown eyes rolled up to look at me mournfully.

I snatched the shoe before he could change his mind. "Don't give me that face," I said. "You are in *so* much trouble."

"Rrrrowwrrrorf?" Tombo said, sounding kind of like Scooby-Doo. He pawed at my knee and managed to look even sadder.

I couldn't stand it. I put my arms around his neck

and hugged him. "Well, *I'm* not the one who's going to be really mad about this," I said. "So don't think you're all forgiven yet. You'll have to try those puppy-dog eyes on Mom and Dad."

"Michelle?" Mom pushed open my door, looking sleepy. She was wearing one of my dad's old T-shirts and blue-green-yellow-striped flannel pants. "Are you all right? Did you fall out of bed?"

"Mom, I haven't done that since second grade," I said. "No, it was, uh . . . Tombo woke me."

Mom squinted at the dog and he wriggled away from me and danced over to her, all excited about having more people awake to play with him.

I really, really, *really* wanted to hide the shoe and act as confused as everyone else when Dad found it missing, but I knew that would be wrong, and Tombo and I would only get in even more trouble later.

So I held the shoe out to Mom and tried to make my "sorry" face as convincing as Tombo's. "He was chewing on this. I'm sorry! I didn't know he would do that!"

Mom's eyes widened. She was really awake now. She came in and took the shoe from my hand, opening and closing her mouth without saying anything. Tombo jumped around her feet, trying to grab the shoe back, but she held it up and put her other hand out flat in front of his face, which actually made him stop jumping. I'd have to remember that.

"Oh, dear," Mom said. She turned the shoe over like she was hoping from a different angle it would turn out to be something else.

"What's going on in here?" Dad asked, appearing in the doorway. "Why are we all up so early? Does this — *what is that?*" His face went long and shocked-looking as Mom handed him his shoe and he stared at the damage.

"He didn't mean to!" I cried. "Maybe he was hungry! Or he got confused! He won't do it again!"

Deandre came out of his room, looking bleary. He took one look at my dad and figured out what had happened.

"Um," he said. "Why don't I take Tombo for a run around the yard?" My brother grabbed Tombo's collar and hustled the dog down the stairs. I'm not sure which conflict resolution technique that was, but it seemed like a good one to me.

"Honey," Mom said to Dad. She put her hands on his shoulders and steered him back to his room. "Let's go back to bed and deal with this later, when you've calmed down."

Dad looked pretty calm to me. Eerily way *too* calm, actually. But he just nodded and they shut their bedroom door behind them.

Well, *I* couldn't go back to sleep. All of my worries about having to give up Tombo were starting to come back. I got dressed and tied up my hair in a bright pink scarf with dark raspberries and blackberries on it. Rosie gave it to me for my last birthday, and I knew it was her favorite of my scarves, although I didn't like it quite as much as the ones I got in Kenya because it didn't feel as soft and it wasn't as long. But maybe it would put her in a good mood if she saw me wearing it, and then she'd be more likely to like Tombo.

I ran downstairs and out into the garden, where Deandre was running in long, steady strides around the perimeter with Tombo loping beside him. I sat down on the back steps to watch them. Dad is always talking about building a deck out here one summer, and Mom keeps saying that one day she'll learn about gardening and plant some flowers, but they've always been too busy, so right now it's just a big patch of green surrounded by a tall white fence. Which meant more room for Tombo to run, at least.

Deandre is trying out for track and field this year, so he'd been practicing his long-distance running all summer. It looked hot and boring to me, but Tombo seemed to love it. His ears flapped back as he ran and he kept glancing up at Deandre like, *This is so cool! How far do you think we've gone? How long until we get there?* I bet he hadn't noticed that they were running in circles.

After another few minutes, Deandre slowed down and jogged over to me. Tombo's eyes lit up when he saw me. He came galloping over and tried to throw his whole body into my lap, which as you might imagine wasn't the best idea. I fended him off and patted my hair to make sure my scarf was still in place.

"Don't worry about it," Deandre said, reading my face. "Dad won't stay mad, and it's not your fault. These things happen with dogs."

"Well, they better not happen again!" I said to Tombo. He wrinkled his forehead quizzically and wagged his butt some more.

"I bet Mom and Dad would cheer up if we made them breakfast," Deandre suggested. "I think I saw a pumpkin pancake mix in the cupboard."

See, I don't know why Rosie complains about her

older brothers so much. If you ask me, mine is pretty cool — you know, most of the time anyway. I don't know if he knew this would happen, but making pumpkin pancakes cheered *me* up a lot too.

Just to be safe, I moved all the shoes from the rack into the hall closet, where Tombo couldn't get at them. And I kept an eye on him the whole time we were in the kitchen. He flopped on the red tile floor under our feet, lurching to his paws whenever he heard an odd noise. The good thing, though, is that he didn't seem to be very barky. Buttons could yap and yap when she had something to say; Tombo just went "Hrrruff?" in a low, puzzled voice and wrinkled his forehead at me.

Mom and Dad came down when they smelled the pancakes, and over breakfast we talked very sensibly about how to keep shoes away from Tombo and rearrange things so he wouldn't be tempted again. They listened to our ideas and asked us what we thought of theirs. I like it when we have conversations like that, because Mom and Dad talk to us as if we're grown-ups just like them.

"All right," Mom said at the end, "so we have a plan to protect the shoes. We can make this work."

We all nodded and there was a small pause.

"But why did it have to be *my* shoe?" Dad said plaintively.

"I guess you have the tastiest feet," Deandre joked, and that made us all laugh. Tombo looked up from his kibble with a scrunched-up, befuddled expression like, *What? What's so funny?*

"So, Michelle, what's going on with your classroom's big project?" Dad asked. He was talking about Ms. Applebaum's "Make a Difference" project. At the beginning of the year, we all had to come up with an idea that would help the community or make the world a better place. I'd remembered something my Kenyan grandma told me about charities that give a goat or a cow to a family in Africa. Apparently just one animal like that could change their lives so much that the kids could afford to go to school and have a totally better life, which sounded amazing to me.

So my suggestion was that we raise enough money to buy a goat for an African family, and everybody loved it, especially Ms. Applebaum. We had a bake sale that raised nearly a hundred dollars, and we were planning to spend the next Saturday raking leaves for people who would pay us for it, so we'd have that money too. But the goat part itself was my responsibility, and I had no idea where to start.

"Good," I said in answer to my dad's question. "I mean, we're working on it. Just a few details to figure out." I knew I could ask him for help if I needed it. But I kind of wanted to figure this out for myself, if I could.

The phone rang and I lunged to answer it, nearly tripping over Tombo, who bolted out of the room as if I'd dropped a grenade on his head.

"Hello?" I said into the receiver.

"Hey!" It was Rosie's voice. I smiled. I realized I hadn't actually expected her to call me, even though she'd said she would.

"Hi Rosie!"

Deandre rolled his eyes and got up to clear the table. I took the portable phone into the den, where Tombo was rolling on his back on the couch. I noticed that he was leaving little brown hairs all over the white leather. I hoped Mom and Dad wouldn't be too upset about that. The boxer looked positively gleeful as he knocked our burnt orange throw pillows onto the floor. The matching blanket on the back of the couch was all crumpled into a corner of the cushions.

"Do you still want to go to the park today?" Rosie asked. "Miguel said he'd walk over with me. I know he's just looking for cheerleaders, but we can ditch him and hang out in the dog run with Buttons. Want to?"

"Sure!" I said. "I'm so excited for you to meet Tombo!" Tombo sat up when he heard his name and tilted his head at me.

"Who?" she said.

"My dog! You'll love him."

"Oh, right," Rosie said, as if she'd forgotten our whole conversation yesterday. "Your dog. Right. You're sure he'll be nice to Buttons?"

"Of course!" I said. I hadn't even thought to worry about that. I sat down on the arm of the couch and tugged on one of the blanket tassels nervously. Tombo buried his nose between two couch cushions and started to root around, making grunting noises.

"OK," she said. "See you there in an hour?"

"Awesome," I said. I hung up and looked down at Tombo. Suddenly the big playdate I'd been looking forward to was filling me with dread instead. Would Tombo be good? What if Buttons didn't like him after all?

What if my whole plan was a failure?

CHAPTER 7

Deandre and I got to the dog run first. There was an older couple at the far end with a small terrier mutt, but they left through the other gate before we got Tombo's leash off, so we had the whole place to ourselves. It was chilly and gray and windy, but sometimes the sun would peek through the clouds, and it didn't feel like it was about to rain. Fallen red leaves rustled under our shoes and collected wetly in the fountain area.

Tombo went galloping around again like he had the day before, with his long legs flying out giddily. He kept stopping to look at Deandre as if he expected another tennis ball to appear, but we weren't going to make that mistake again!

"Come here, Tombo!" I called. He tossed his head up so his ears flapped, sat down by the water fountain, and grinned at me. I made a mental note that we'd have to work on that. It would be too embarrassing to have a dog who didn't come when he was called.

The gate squeaked behind us. I whirled around, all excited to see Rosie and Buttons, but my smile fell off my face as I saw who was coming through the gate with them.

Yup. *Pippa*. Why was she here? Rosie hadn't said anything about inviting her!

I forced the smile back on my face and waved. "Hey guys!"

Suddenly a blur of brown fur shot past me. Tombo rocketed up to Buttons, knocked her over with his square snout, and planted one big paw on her tiny underbelly.

Rosie shrieked like she was the one being sniffed all over by something ten times her size. "Help!" she yelled. "That dog's going to eat Buttons!" She tried to shove Tombo off the poodle puppy, but he just gave her a *Who the heck are you?* look and stayed planted in place.

"He's not going to eat her!" I said, running up to them. At least, I was pretty sure he wouldn't do that. Miss Hameed would have told us if he had trouble with other dogs. Wouldn't she? Besides, Buttons was pawing cheerfully at his nose and trying to chew his jowls, so *she* didn't seem that upset. I grabbed Tombo's collar and yanked him away from Buttons.

Immediately Buttons sprang up and tried to jump at Tombo's face. Her small puff of a tail was wagging frantically and she let out little yips as she pounced on his paws.

"See?" I said. "She's totally fine. She likes him!"

"He might have hurt her!" Rosie cried. She scooped Buttons up and cuddled the puppy close to her neck. "It's all right, sweetie, you're OK now," she cooed. Buttons seriously gave her a look like, *Well, yeah, of course I am. Why wouldn't I be?*

Behind her, her older brother Miguel rolled his eyes. "Rosie, there's no need to act hysterical," he said.

"I'm not being hysterical!" Rosie said, her voice going up and up. "I just want to protect my puppy!"

"You don't need to protect her from Tombo," I said. "He's really friendly. Just look at his face."

Tombo wagged his whole butt and beamed at Rosie and Buttons.

Rosie stared at me for a minute. Her black curls were pinned back with two pink butterfly barrettes and she was wearing her second-favorite pink sweater.

I bet Pippa didn't even know the order of Rosie's favorite pink things like I did. Pippa was standing quietly a little ways away, watching Rosie nervously. Her long blond hair kept blowing in her face and she unbuttoned and buttoned the last button of her gray cardigan over and over again.

"Tombo?" Rosie echoed. "Wait. *This* . . . this *gigantic beast* . . . is your new dog?"

Of course that made me mad. I mean, it's just basic psychology, not to mention manners: You never insult someone's family and you especially never insult their dog. I'd never had a dog before, but even I knew that!

"He's not a gigantic beast!" I said. "He's a boxer! And he's a good dog!"

Deandre made a little snorting noise and I shot him a death glare. Tombo grinned up at me like, *Well, we don't have to tell her the WHOLE truth.*

"You didn't tell me you got a big slobbery shedding dog!" Rosie said. "I thought you got another cute little dog like Buttons! So they could be friends!"

"Tombo and Buttons can be friends," I said. "She loves playing with any dog, no matter what size they are."

"Sure, maybe *she* does, but what if he squashes her by accident or something?" Rosie demanded. "With his great galumphing paws?"

"Jeez, Rosie, she's a puppy. She's not made of glass," Miguel chimed in. Now it was his turn to get a death glare. He held up his hands like he was surrendering. "I'm staying out of this. Deandre, want to go to the lake?"

"Yeah, OK." Miguel is a year older than my brother, but they've hung out a lot because of Rosie and me, so they're friends in that way guys are where they don't call each other, but they always seem cool with seeing each other. Deandre tugged lightly on my pink hair scarf. "Don't go anywhere," he said. "I'll be back soon."

"Yeah, and no fighting, girls," Miguel said, as if he were a hundred years older than us and all wise about friendships and the universe and everything. I think Rosie and I both wanted to kick him right then.

Neither of us said anything as the guys went out the gate. Rosie was still clutching Buttons to her, but the puppy was starting to wriggle like she really wanted to get down and play. She made a little frustrated whimpering noise and stared at Tombo.

"Just let them play," I said. "You'll see. They'll have fun, I swear."

Rosie looked over at Pippa. That made me mad too. Like suddenly Pippa was the person she asked for advice? What did Pippa know about anything? Especially dogs?

Pippa tucked her hair behind her ear and stubbed her sneaker against the ground. "It seems OK to me," she said softly. "I mean, it looks like Buttons really wants to play."

Well, OK. At least she was on my side for once.

Rosie sighed dramatically. "Fine, but I'm watching him!" she said.

My temper flared, but I held my tongue. Dad always says that when you're mad, you should stop and think through what you're going to say and how you want the other person to react. Like, don't just say the first thing that pops into your head. I'm not very good at this, but I try!

I hung on to Tombo's collar as Rosie gently set Buttons down on the ground. The moment she let go, Buttons barreled over to Tombo and stood up on her hind legs, trying to paw at his face. I let go of Tombo, and he did a funny little dance with his front paws, bending over like he was bowing with his butt up in the air and his stubby tail waving madly. Buttons squeaked with delight and batted his nose.

Tombo scrunched himself all the way down until his head was lower than hers and his whole body was pressed into the ground. He wriggled closer to her like he was saying, *See, I'm not so big! I'm not scary at all! I can be little like you!*

"Ruff!" Buttons yipped, jumping back and shaking herself so her white fur puffed out. She pounced on Tombo's massive head and flopped across his face like she thought she was pinning him down.

Tombo pawed cautiously at the fuzzy thing clinging to his face, and then he stretched himself out and rolled over, exposing his pale pink and white underbelly. Buttons rolled with him, and as her paws hit the ground on the other side of his head, she let out a little yelp.

Rosie darted forward with a horrified gasp and snatched her up. Both Tombo and Buttons looked confused.

"See?" Rosie said to me. "He's too big to play with her!"

"That's crazy!" I said. "Buttons was having fun! She likes him!"

Rosie was busy inspecting each of Buttons' paws

carefully, looking for injuries in a fussy, melodramatic way. Buttons licked Rosie's ear and then pressed her front paws against the side of Rosie's face, pushing her away like she was saying, *Sheesh, Mom, I'm FINE; can I please go PLAY now?*

Rosie shook her head. "I just can't believe you chose a dog like that," she said to me. "Was it Deandre? Did he pick it? I know how brothers are. And you don't stand up to yours the way I do to mine."

In a flash, I saw what I could do — what I *ought* to do — to stay Rosie's friend. If I told her the boxer was Deandre's idea, I knew exactly what would happen. I could picture the sympathetic look on her face and the way she'd squeeze my hand as we talked about how awful big brothers are. She'd nod and listen with her black curls bobbing as I told her about all the trouble Tombo had caused already and how worried I was about him being a bad dog. She'd gasp and giggle about Dad's shoe. And then she'd pat my shoulder and tell me I could come play with Buttons anytime I felt too overwhelmed by "Deandre's dog."

It would work. It would be perfect. And all I had to do to make this dream of friendship unfold was betray Tombo.

I looked down at his sweet, confused face. He wouldn't even know. "I — I guess — maybe —" I said.

"I knew it!" Rosie stuck out her tongue at Tombo. "I knew you wouldn't pick a dog like that yourself. But you're too nice, Michelle, letting Deandre make all the decisions. I've always said I'd never let my brothers push me around like that."

I was already feeling guilty, and like I'd somehow betrayed Deandre too. "Well, I mean, I don't actually —"

"It's too bad they left already," Rosie said, glancing around, "or else we could make them take Tombo with them. Then we could play with Buttons without worrying about him."

"They could still play . . ." I started to say, but trailed off at the stubborn look on Rosie's face.

"I brought a tennis ball to throw for her," Rosie said. "It is the *cutest* thing watching her fetch it. That'll be way more fun than the two of them playing anyway, even if it wasn't totally dangerous too."

After Tombo's performance the day before, I couldn't exactly suggest throwing the ball for both of them. Rosie would be furious if he destroyed her tennis ball. But it didn't seem fair. Even Buttons looked much more interested in Tombo than playing with us.

Tombo crouched down a little lower and gave Rosie a pleading look. To me, it was like his good intentions were written all over his face. Why couldn't she see that like I could?

"I know," Rosie said in her queen-of-the-playground voice. "Michelle, put his leash on him and tie him to the fence. That way he'll have to stay put while we play with Buttons."

I met Tombo's eyes and felt horrible. "But —"

"Right, Pippa?" Rosie said. "That's what we should do, isn't it?"

Pippa lifted one shoulder and looked anxious. "Um, sure, I guess."

"It's not like he'll care," Rosie said. "He'll probably just go to sleep, like Meatball does in our agility classes. He probably won't even notice the difference."

I knew that wasn't true. I knew exactly how poor Tombo would feel — left out, just like I did when Rosie hung out with Pippa and didn't invite me. He'd feel unwanted and tossed aside. He'd be desperate to play with us and Buttons, and he'd be heartbroken that we weren't including him.

Tombo poked my hand with his nose. His chocolate-brown eyes asked me why he couldn't play with the funny little dog. The wrinkles in his forehead seemed to be saying *Why are we all so tense? What are we worrying about? Can I help? Can I fix it?*

"This isn't fair," I said. I could hear Dad's voice in my head saying *"Stop and think through how you want them to react!"* But that didn't help, because right then I just wanted to make Rosie as mad as she was making me.

"You're being so mean to Tombo without even giving him a chance," I said. "He wants to be a good dog! Even Buttons knows that! You're the only one judging him by his size instead of his character, which is exactly what you're always complaining people do about small dogs, so you should know better. And for your information, *I* picked him, not Deandre. I picked him because he's sweet and good, and I love him, and he's much nicer and more loyal than you are anyway, Rosie Sanchez!"

Rosie's mouth dropped open. "What are you talking about?" she cried. "I'm not mean at all! I'm nice! I'm your friend!"

"Oh, yeah?" I said. "Because lately it seems like you're Pippa's friend and nobody else's."

Pippa turned bright pink. She and Rosie both looked completely astonished, as if I'd just accused them of being Martians or something.

"I thought all *three* of us were friends," Rosie said.

"No, you thought I was your extra friend, for spare whenever Pippa's not around. Well, not anymore!" I said. I clipped Tombo's leash onto his collar. "Come on, Tombo, we know where we're not wanted."

I tried to march angrily out of the dog run, but it was hard because Tombo kept stopping to gaze back at Buttons or trying to lurch back toward her, and I ended up having to drag him through the gates. So it wasn't quite the dramatic exit I wanted.

I also realized as the gate clanged behind me that Deandre had told me to stay there. But I couldn't go back after that, could I? I'd have to go look for him at the lake.

"We told her, didn't we, Tombo?" I said as we headed down the path. My dog shook himself and tried to catch a flying leaf in his mouth. He was happy again now that we were together. Maybe he'd even forgotten about Buttons already.

He had no idea that he'd just caused the biggest fight I'd ever had with my best friend.

CHAPTER 8

The wind felt like it was getting colder as I walked under the yellow and orange trees toward the lake. I wrapped the leash around one wrist and stuck my hands in the pockets of my dark red fleece jacket. I wished I'd remembered to bring gloves. It was only October twelfth, but thick gray clouds were piling up in front of the sun and hiding its warmth.

Tombo loved the wind. He jumped around like a crazy thing every time a leaf whipped past his nose and he kept spinning to stare at the bushes when they creaked and rustled.

I'd only gone halfway down the path when I started feeling terrible. At first I was really proud of myself for standing up for Tombo. But then the fight had turned into something else. When it was about our dogs, I knew I was right to defend him. But although I'd been thinking all those thoughts about our friendship for months, I wasn't sure I should have said them out loud. Especially in front of Pippa. I didn't mean to make *her* feel bad.

I just wanted Rosie to see how she'd changed and to start treating me like her best friend again. In my head, when this was all fixed, Pippa could still hang out with us. It's just that Rosie used to call me first and tell me everything. And now I felt like the elephant who was trying so hard to be friends with a pair of zebras, but who didn't fit into their group anymore.

I brushed away tears and blew on my hands to warm them up. Had Rosie really not noticed that things were different? Did she think we were all getting along perfectly?

Was *I* the one causing problems?

Maybe Dad was right. Maybe I should have spent more time thinking before I started yelling at her. How would we ever fix things now? What if I'd lost my best friend for real this time? Who would I sit with at lunch?

But I couldn't have done what she wanted me to do to Tombo anyway. And the way she'd acted toward my poor dog just made me so *mad*.

As I had that thought, Tombo braked and twisted his head to look alertly off at the low hill on the left side of the path. His whole body was poised like he was ready for action. His face was clearly trying to say *I'm on top of things! Nothing gets past me!* but the funny wrinkles in his forehead and his drooping jowls made him look a bit too goofy to take seriously. I smiled, thinking *At least I have one friend who'll like me no matter what I say.*

Suddenly Tombo bolted. He took off so fast that the leash whipped out of my hand. I barely had time to shout, "Tombo, no! Come back!" before he'd disappeared up the hill and over the other side.

I ran after him. My heart pounded in my chest. I couldn't have lost my dog already! I had promised to be responsible and take care of him!

A tree branch whacked me in the face, but I kept running. At the top of the hill, the trees stopped in a ragged line. The other side of the hill swooped down a long way to an open, grassy field, on the same level as the lake, which I could see not far off to my right, shielded by more trees.

Tombo was galloping down the hill, bobbing through the grass like an overgrown brown jackrabbit. In the field I could see something long and gray racing back and forth. My first, panicked thought was that it might be a wolf, although I'd never heard of anyone seeing wolves around here. But it moved so gracefully and quickly, and I was already so afraid for Tombo, that "wolf" flashed through my head before I could think sensibly.

I charged down the hill after Tombo, staggering on the uneven dirt and unexpected mounds under the grass. It was steeper than I'd realized, and soon I was going faster than I meant to, but I couldn't stop myself.

As we got closer, I realized that the gray running creature was a dog — but a huge dog, long-legged and sleek and silvery like someone had turned the moon into a dog. Under its short, silver-gray fur, I could see strong muscles rippling across its chest and back as it ran.

Tombo barked once, a ringing, *Hey, look out below, I'm coming to say hi!* kind of bark.

The other dog slowed to a lope and trotted in a big circle, watching Tombo approach. My dog looked like such a galumphing clown in comparison to this dog's casual grace. I hoped it was friendly. I hoped it could tell that Tombo was not a threat.

My sneaker caught on a hole in the ground and I went flying, tumbling head over heels the rest of the way down the hill. I landed with a thud in the long grass, sprawled out on my stomach. Tombo, my so-called loyal friend, didn't even come over to check if I was OK. When I managed to catch my breath enough to sit up, he was bowing and dancing in front of the gray dog the way he had for Buttons.

The gray dog looked intrigued and thoughtful, but not unfriendly. Its tail was longer than Tombo's — maybe the length of my arm, wrist to elbow, and round at the tip — and it was wagging in a way that made me feel much better.

I rubbed my head and retied my scarf around my hair. My left ankle felt a little sore. I was about to try standing on it when I heard footsteps running up to me.

"It's Michelle!" cried a familiar voice. I looked up and saw Satoshi and Midori skidding to a stop beside me. Today Satoshi was wearing green and black, while Midori had on a candy-cane-striped sweater with her jeans.

"Are you OK?" Midori asked. She sounded out of breath and her two pigtails were coming loose.

"Yeah, I'm fine," I said. "I think." I started to climb to my feet, and to my surprise Satoshi took my hand and helped me up. Gingerly I tested putting some weight on my left ankle. It hurt a little, but I could stand on it, so it was probably just bruised.

Now finally Tombo came back to check on me, although mostly he wanted to say hi to the new people. He nosed Midori's hand and she patted his head with a smile.

The gray dog slipped quietly up between Midori and Satoshi and presented its head for petting as well. I caught myself wondering what Rosie would say if she saw me hanging out with the Takashi twins and two big dogs. Not that I cared anymore or anything.

"I guess this is your dog?" I asked them.

"Yeah," Satoshi said. "She needs to run a *lot*, so we bring her here whenever we can." He waved at the empty field around us.

"There's more space than the dog run, and usually we have it all to ourselves," Midori explained. "Sorry we got your dog all excited, though!" She handed the end of Tombo's leash back to me.

I held out my other hand for the gray dog to sniff. She had a long nose and long flapping ears like a beagle's, but more square. Her eyes were the weirdest color blue. I didn't think I'd ever seen blue eyes on a dog before. "What's her name?" I asked.

"Chihiro," Satoshi said.

"It's from my favorite movie," Midori added quickly.

I stared at her in surprise. "You don't mean *Spirited Away*, do you?"

Her eyebrows went up, and she smiled. "You know it?"

"Know it? I *love* it!" I said. I'd had no idea there were other Miyazaki fans in my class. "My dog's name is Tombo!"

"From *Kiki's Delivery Service*!" Midori exclaimed. Her smile went from ear to ear now. "That is so cool! Have you seen all his movies?"

"Of course!" I said.

"Uh-oh. This could go on all day," Satoshi said, shaking his head and grinning. "I'm going to run Chihiro a bit more. Want me to take Tombo too?"

"I'm not sure yet how good he is off-leash," I said. "Like, if he'll come back when I call and stuff. I'm guessing no."

"That's OK, I'll hang on to him," Satoshi said. He took the leash from my hand and wrapped it firmly around his own. His hair was cut straight and even all around his head and he usually had a serious expression, but with a big dog on either side of him, he looked like a young warrior from an anime movie.

The three of them ran off into the field and Midori and I sat down in the grass to watch and talk about our favorite movies. At first Chihiro stayed at Satoshi's pace, but soon she put on a burst of speed and tore ahead. Tombo tried to lunge after her, but Satoshi kept him close to his side. A minute later, Chihiro came bounding back and started to tease Tombo, running at him and then darting back, making small playful barks and wagging her tail.

"That's so cute," I said. "I think they like each other."

"Yeah, and Chihiro can be fussy, so Tombo should be flattered," Midori said.

"She has the coolest eyes," I said. "What kind of dog is she? I feel like I've seen dogs like that in photos, like on calendars and stuff."

Midori nodded. "There's a famous photographer named William Wegman who takes lots of pictures of these kinds of dogs. They're called Weimaraners."

"She's gorgeous," I said.

"So is yours!" Midori said. "I love boxers. They're so full of energy."

I kind of wanted to hug Midori right then, although of course I didn't. But that was exactly the reaction I had wanted from Rosie. Of course my dog was gorgeous! And lovable! Rosie was blind if she couldn't see that.

I looked sideways at Midori. Maybe Rosie had been all wrong about her, too. Maybe she wasn't a tomboy or boy-crazy. Maybe she just didn't have any girl friends because the girls in our class didn't talk to her — not the other way around.

Well, she seemed nice, and I didn't care what Rosie thought. "Hey," I said, "maybe sometime you could bring Chihiro over to my house to play with Tombo. We have a big, fenced backyard . . . I mean, if you want to . . . it could be fun."

"Sure!" Midori said. "I have swim practice after school tomorrow, and Tuesday I have to be home by five for my cello lesson, but maybe before five would work? Or Wednesday?"

"I'll check with my parents," I said. "Uh-oh." Talking about the time made me realize that Deandre might be looking for me. "What time is it?"

Midori looked at her watch, which had a grumpy-looking cartoon penguin on its round face. "Almost noon," she said.

"I'd better go find my brother," I said, climbing to my feet. Satoshi saw me stand up and came running back with Tombo. The boxer's long pink tongue was lolling out of the side of his mouth and his face was lit up with joy.

"Thanks for playing with him," I said to Satoshi.

"No problem. He's cool," Satoshi said with a shrug.

"I'll talk to you tomorrow, OK?" I said to Midori.

"Sure," she said. "I mean, if you can. If you don't, it's all right."

I didn't realize what an odd thing that was to say until I was halfway across the field to the lake. What did she mean by that? Like, if I decided I didn't want to hang out with her, she'd understand? That wouldn't be very nice of me. But she'd said it with a perfectly friendly smile on her face.

Maybe Midori's psychology was more complicated than I'd realized. I'd have to pay attention if we were going to be friends.

Then again . . . were we going to be friends? I didn't know her that well yet. What if she didn't really want to be friends with me? Maybe we had nothing in common besides big dogs and Miyazaki movies. But on the plus side, being friends with someone new would certainly show Rosie I didn't need her. Unless then Rosie decided she would never take me back because I'd spent too much time with weirdos.

I glanced down at Tombo and he wagged his stumpy tail. "I bet I can guess who you'd vote for," I said. "But you just want to spend more time with Chihiro."

His face said, *So? She's awesome! Let's go back and play with her some more right now!*

I sighed. Friends were complicated. I wished I knew how to handle them as easily as Tombo handled his new dog friends.

"Well, I'll figure it out tomorrow," I said to Tombo. "For the rest of today, it's just you and me, partner."

He looked pleased, as if he'd understood me.

Little did I know that my troubles with Tombo were far from over.

CHAPTER 9

I found Deandre skipping stones at the lake with Miguel. I think they might have been talking about girls, too, because they both shut up really fast when I showed up. My brother looked surprised to see me, but on the walk home I explained about the fight with Rosie.

Deandre shook his head. "I'm not sure that was the way to handle it," he said.

"I know," I said, kicking a pile of orange leaves into the gutter. "I didn't think through what I was going to say. I didn't go into the argument with my goals in mind. I did all the things Dad is always telling me not to."

Deandre squeezed my shoulder. "Still," he said, "I think I probably would have done the same thing you did."

I looked up at him. "Really?"

"Not that that makes it right," he said. "But poor Tombo!"

"Exactly!" I said. "Poor Tombo."

Poor Tombo looked like he was having the time of his life. He flung himself into every pile of leaves and lunged to the end of his leash whenever he saw someone on the other side of the street. He darted back and forth so much that he got me and Deandre tangled up in the leash and we had to keep stopping to unwrap ourselves.

When we got home, Mom and Dad were making tuna melts and salad for lunch. My tuna melt had fake cheese on it, because I'm lactose-intolerant, which means too much of anything with milk makes me sick.

Tombo flopped out on the kitchen floor and fell asleep right away.

"That's a sign of a happy dog," Dad said, smiling. "Did he have fun with Buttons?"

"He tried to," I said. "Rosie wouldn't let them play for long. But he met this other dog called Chihiro who's really cool — she belongs to my friend Midori." It sounded weird to say "my friend Midori," even though I'd technically known her since we moved to town in second grade. "So I was wondering if they could maybe come over for the dogs to play together on Tuesday after school. Would that be OK?"

Mom pulled her appointment book out of her purse and flipped through it. She comes home early on Tuesdays and Fridays to be here when we get out of school, and Dad does the same thing Mondays and Thursdays. On Wednesdays Deandre stays late at school, usually for sports stuff, and I almost always go to Rosie's mom's store with her and Pippa. I wondered what I would do this Wednesday if Rosie and I were still fighting.

"Sounds like a good idea," Mom said, making a note in her book in pencil. "How do you spell Midori?" I spelled it for her. Mom likes to write everything down. She's a little more organized than my dad that way.

"Grandpa called to invite us for dinner," Dad said. "If you guys are done with your homework."

"Yup," said Deandre, and I nodded too, although I hadn't figured out the goat-giving part of our project yet. But that wasn't really *homework*. That was just Ms. Applebaum asking me to find her some information about donating goats. She hadn't given me a deadline for that or anything.

Grandma and Grandpa (my mom's parents) live

fifteen minutes away, in the next town over, so we see them a lot. Definitely more than my other grandparents, who live in Kenya — we've only been to visit them three times, because it's really expensive to fly there, but when we went we stayed for a month each time.

I loved everything about Kenya; I loved the heat, and the monkeys in the trees around the farm, and the bright, colorful dresses my grandmother wears, and milking her goats and cows, and reading to each other by candlelight when the power went off in the middle of the night.

But I love my American grandparents too. Their basement is one big library of old books, which my grandmother collects, and she lets me borrow the ones that aren't too antique. Grandpa decided to learn to be a cook after he retired, so he took all these classes and now he's really good and he won't even let Grandma in the kitchen. It's pretty funny. She keeps saying how much easier her life would have been if he'd done this years ago, and wondering if he decided to do this because she is such a terrible cook — which is true, actually. I didn't know you could make beans and rice or pancakes completely wrong until I tasted Grandma's.

"Can we bring Tombo?" I asked. "I bet they'd love to meet him!"

Mom and Dad exchanged looks. "I bet they would too," Dad said, "but think about how small and cluttered their house is."

"I agree," Mom said. "I'm afraid he'd break something or make a mess — it might be better if we wait to introduce them here or during the day, when we can leave him in their yard."

I was disappointed, but I couldn't argue with that. Every surface in their house is covered in little knick-knacks and cute ornaments. It would be way too easy for a big, excitable dog to knock something over, and I wanted Grandma and Grandpa to meet Tombo in whatever way would make sure they liked him.

We spent almost the whole rest of the afternoon trying to decide what to do with Tombo while we were gone. Dad suggested leaving him in the big crate we'd gotten for him, but I was afraid he'd be sad if we locked him up in there. I thought he'd be fine if we left him loose in the house. After all, we'd hidden all the shoes! Deandre laughed at that idea, and said we could do what we liked, but *he'd* be leaving his door shut, just to make sure his stuff was safe.

What finally convinced Mom and Dad was that

Tombo was so good and quiet all afternoon. He was so tired from our walk and playing in the park that he slept for hours and didn't act crazy at all. My mom said maybe chewing on Dad's shoe was just first-day nerves, but now he'd settle down and be good.

So we compromised. We left Tombo shut into the kitchen and den area. With the doors closed, he wouldn't be able to get to the rest of the house. But he'd still be able to get to his food and water in the kitchen, or go sleep on the sofa in the den if he wanted to — I know that's what I would do! And we wouldn't be gone long. Dad said it would be a good test, since we had to leave him home alone the next day while we were all at school or work.

"Be good, Tombo!" I said, patting his head. I'd changed into one of the scarves Grandma had given me, bright red with a swirling gold dragon and little dangling gold beads on the ends. Rosie's pink scarf was stuffed into the back of my closet, under my pile of socks that don't match and my soccer uniform from summer camp. Looking at those raspberries just made me mad at Rosie all over again.

I guess part of me thought she might call and say she was sorry, but hours had passed and I hadn't heard from her. Which was just fine. If Pippa was enough of a friend for Rosie, then she could have her and her dumb cat, who would never be as awesome as Tombo.

Tombo sat up and looked confused as we all got ready to leave. He tried to follow me out of the kitchen, but I said, "No, Tombo. Stay! Be good!" and shut the door on him.

"Rooooooooooorrrrrrooooooooorrrrr," he whimpered, scrabbling on the other side of the door. "Ooooorrrroooo? Aarrrrrroooooo!"

I clutched my heart. "So sad!" I whispered to Mom and Dad. "Poor Tombo!"

"He'll settle down once we're gone," Dad whispered back, handing me my shoes.

I hoped Dad was right. I could still hear Tombo making sad little whimpering noises as we went out the front door.

Grandpa's dinner helped me forget about Rosie for a while. He made chicken piccata with mushrooms over spaghetti, plus homemade honey-wheat bread and grilled zucchini. We'd gotten him a bread machine for his last birthday, but it was more of a present for us because now he made fresh bread all the time, and their whole house smelled amazing.

I told Grandma all about our "Make a Difference" project and buying a goat, which she thought was a wonderful idea. Except then she started asking me which charity we were using to get the goat, and I remembered that I was supposed to be figuring that out. All I could do was mumble, "We're working on that part." I hoped Ms. Applebaum wouldn't ask me about it at school the next day.

Still, I was in a much better mood when we got back home. Dad switched on the light in the living room, and immediately we heard frantic scrabbling noises coming from the kitchen door.

"He's happy to see us!" I said, smiling. "Isn't it great to come home to that kind of excitement?"

But what we found behind the door wasn't great at all.

Tombo threw himself at us the minute the door opened, so it wasn't until we'd said hi to him and wrestled him back down to the floor that we saw what he'd done.

Tombo's food bowl was upside down and kibble was scattered from one end of the kitchen to the other, most of it soggy and gross from the puddle spreading out from the tipped-over water bowl. All the dish towels he could reach had been dragged off their hooks and shredded. Two of the wooden chairs around the table had deep tooth marks on their legs, as if Tombo had been gnawing on them.

"Uh-oh," Deandre said, jumping over the puddle and running into the den. Tombo bounded after him with a cheerful face like, *Yay! What game is this?*

The destruction in here was even worse. The orange throw pillows were ripped open and all the feathers inside were drifting around the room. The remote control for the TV was on the floor, cracked and chewed into a black plastic mess. Tombo had even pulled one of the big glossy books off the low shelf under the coffee table and nibbled on all the corners. Worst of all, he'd left long gouges and big slobbery bites in the arm of the leather couch.

"Oh. My. Gosh," I said. I sat down on one of the armchairs, feeling faint. My mom looked as horrified as I felt. Dad went over to the couch and gingerly touched the leather like he couldn't believe it was real. Deandre picked up the remote and pointed it at the TV, but of course it didn't work.

"This is bad," Deandre said, and I knew he wasn't just talking about how he'd miss *The Amazing Race* that night.

"Tombo," I said. The boxer looked at me, and then

his head drooped and his shoulders slumped and he made the saddest face I'd ever seen. He knew we were very, very unhappy with him.

"Oh, Tombo," I said. "I thought you were a good dog."

He peered up at me with his big brown eyes. *I am!* they said. *I mean, I try to be. What did I do wrong?*

I shook my head. Mom and Dad sighed and went to put their coats away. Deandre opened the broom closet to get a vacuum cleaner for the feathers.

"This isn't something a good dog would do," I told Tombo. He ducked his head even more. He did look sorry. But would Mom and Dad ever forgive him? Or would they make us take him back to the shelter?

What if he kept doing things like this? What if he destroyed our whole house?

I thought of something I'd once heard my dad say about a serial killer he was studying. He said there was something so messed up in the guy's brain that psychology couldn't fix him. The phrase he'd used was "bad to the bone."

What if my new dog was too bad to be fixed? What if Tombo was "bad to the bone"?

CHAPTER 10

I didn't dare argue when Mom put Tombo in his crate the next morning. It was a big crate with black metal bars and plenty of room for Tombo to stretch out. We put his fluffy dog bed and blue rope toy and water bowl in there with him. It wasn't so terrible. It even looked kind of comfortable. Still, I didn't think *I'd* want to spend the whole day in a crate.

Tombo tried to hide when he saw the crate and figured out what we were up to. We had to drag him out from behind the sofa and give him lots of treats to get him inside. He hunched his shoulders as we closed the door, then lay down with a sigh. He propped his head on his front paws so his jowls flopped over to either side, whimpered tragically, and gave me enormous puppy dog eyes of woe.

"I'm sorry, Tombo," I said. "But it's for your own good. This way you'll have to be a good dog, because you can't be bad if you're stuck in there."

He sighed again, long and dramatic. I had the uneasy feeling he was thinking, *We'll see about that*.

Mom draped an old towel over the top of the crate. "That should make it feel like more of a den," she said. "What do you think, Tombo? Isn't it nice and cozy in there?"

Tombo practically rolled his eyes at her.

Mom and Dad hadn't said anything about taking him back to the shelter. Maybe they thought he deserved another chance. Or maybe they were looking for a way to break the news to us nicely. Or maybe they felt too guilty to abandon him like his other family had. I certainly wasn't going to give them the idea if they hadn't thought of it themselves! I still had some hope that we'd find a way to fix him.

"I'll stop by at lunchtime and let him out," Mom reassured me as I put on my sunflower-yellow backpack. Deandre had already left to catch the school bus and Dad went to work early on the days when he came home early for us.

"Thanks, Mom," I said. I waved good-bye to Tombo, and he furrowed his brow at me sadly through the bars.

Tombo wasn't the only thing I had to worry about, of course. I didn't know what would happen when

Rosie and I saw each other. I was hoping she would say she was sorry and everything would be all right, but on the other hand, I knew Rosie. She was the most stubborn person I'd ever met. We'd had arguments before, and I couldn't remember her ever being the one to apologize first. Well, I wasn't going to crack this time. For once, she could come to *me*.

There were a bunch of kids in the playground when Mom dropped me off. I saw a flash of pink ribbons and guessed that Rosie was one of them, so I went straight to our classroom instead. Ms. Applebaum was there, writing on the chalkboard. Her big scroll of "Make a Difference" ideas from us hung down on one side of the board, covered in gold star stickers and big smiley faces and pictures of the globe.

Kerri and Emmy Drake were already at their desks, whispering to each other with scowls on their faces, so I guessed that they were fighting again, as usual. My desk was next to Rosie's, with Pippa's on the other side of her; both of them were still empty. Charlie Grayson was in his seat, in the desk in front of mine, drawing spaceships in his notebook. He looked up and smiled at me as I came in. Charlie is short and quiet and never argues with anyone. I've been to his birthday party every year and I still don't know much about him except that he wants to be an astronaut one day.

I took out my math homework and arranged my pencils on my desk. I had enormous butterflies flapping around in my stomach because I was so nervous about seeing Rosie. I jumped a little every time someone came in the door.

But Midori and Satoshi got there before Rosie did. I smiled really big and waved at Midori. She looked a little surprised, but she waved back as she put her book bag down beside her desk in the front row. It wasn't a backpack like most of us had; it was more like a messenger bag, dark gray with apple green accents and a cheerful-looking polar bear key ring hanging off the zipper.

Midori hesitated for a second, glancing at Rosie's empty desk, and then she came over to my desk. Charlie glanced up like he thought she might be coming to talk to him.

"Hey," she said to me. "I love your scarf. I think I've noticed it before."

"Thanks!" I said. "It's the one I always wear for luck." The scarf is dark red with flecks of black and coppery gold, which, if you look at it closely, you can see are sketches of dolphins jumping through waves. I wore it last year when I won our class spelling bee (although Pradesh Mehta won the whole school spelling bee) and again when I was picked for a solo in our chorus recital, and also this year when my "Make a Difference" project was chosen by Ms. Applebaum. It makes me feel like I can do anything. So I was hoping it would help me be strong enough to not talk to Rosie until she talked to me.

"It's really cool," Midori said. "Hey, it kind of matches my shirt." She held out her arm and I realized that under her black sweater, she was wearing a dark red shirt with black vertical stripes.

"It totally does!" I said. The classroom door swept open and I felt a wave of nerves as Rosie burst into the room. Pippa was right behind her, and Rosie, as usual, was talking a mile a minute.

Midori saw my eyes go to them, and she turned to see what I was looking at. When she saw Rosie, she gave me a nod and started to go back to her seat.

"Wait!" I said, grabbing her wrist before she could leave. Charlie looked over his shoulder to give me a mildly puzzled look. Midori looked startled too. "Um," I said. I was trying to think of how to keep her there until class started, but I couldn't just hang on to her like that. "Oh, right," I said, letting go of her. "I meant to tell you, I asked my mom, and she said you and Chihiro can come over tomorrow after school, if you want."

Midori's smile was like one of those scenes in a movie where the pirates open the treasure chest and suddenly all the gold is sparkling and shining and filling the screen. "That would be great!" she said, just as Rosie flounced into her chair across the aisle from me. "Thanks for inviting me."

"Yeah," I said. "It'll be really fun to hang out together." I smiled back at her. I could tell that Rosie was shooting us sideways looks but trying to act like she hadn't noticed I was there.

Luckily, right then the bell rang. Midori hurried back to her seat, and Ms. Applebaum stood up, and then we were handing in our homework and talking about long division and I breathed a sigh of relief. Now I didn't have to worry about Rosie until lunch. She was definitely pretending to ignore me. Her nose was up in the air and she kept turning to whisper to Pippa in a really obvious way, until Ms. Applebaum scolded her for being distracting.

The morning passed like that, kind of uncomfortably, as if a chilly wind were coming from the area to my right. When the bell rang for lunch, Rosie jumped to her feet, grabbed Pippa's arm, and marched out of the classroom with her chin up like she was daring me to come sit with them.

I got my little tiger-print wallet out of my backpack slowly and joined the end of the line going to the cafeteria. Rosie and Pippa went straight to our table like they always do. Pippa brings little Tupperware containers of leftovers from her mom and Rosie always makes her own sandwiches in this fussy, hyper-neat way with the crusts cut off and stuff. I tried to make mine to match hers for a while last year, but it took forever, and anyway, I kind of like the cafeteria food, although I know I might be the only person on the planet who feels that way.

Once I had my flat hamburger and soggy green beans and oatmeal raisin cookie, I stood for a minute with my tray, looking at our table. Rosie's back was to me, but I'm sure she knew I was standing there and I'm sure she was expecting me to come over and beg her forgiveness so I'd have somewhere to sit.

I tossed my lucky scarf back over my shoulder. That wasn't going to happen. I was my own person. I could find somewhere else to sit.

I walked right past Rosie's table and over to where Midori was sitting with Satoshi and Charlie and Arnold Scott. They all looked perfectly astonished when I stopped next to them, as if a giraffe had walked up to their table instead of one of their fellow classmates.

"Hey Midori," I said. "Is it OK if I sit with you guys today?"

Midori blinked a few times, and then she said, "Yeah, of course, sure. Right, guys? That's OK?"

The three boys kind of nodded and shrugged, and Satoshi scooted over so I could sit next to him and across from Midori.

"Thanks," I said. I tried to look like this was totally normal, as if I changed tables every day, but they were all still kind of staring at me like I was nuts. I turned to Charlie, who was sitting next to Midori. "Hey, Charlie, isn't your birthday this weekend?"

"We were just talking about that," Midori said, stealing a carrot from the little bag in front of Satoshi.

Charlie nodded. "But I'm not having a party this year," he said, sounding a bit embarrassed. "I asked my mom if I could have a dog for my birthday, and she said we could if we skipped the party. So we're going to get him next Sunday."

"Um, awesome!" I said. "A dog is better than a party any day! Do you know what kind you're getting?"

"I want a dachshund," he said. "You know, the funny little short dogs."

"They are *so* cute," Midori said.

"But not too cute," Arnold jumped in, leaning over from the other side of Satoshi. "Not like the kind of dog that just sleeps on velvet pillows and eats caviar all day, right, Charlie?"

"Dogs don't eat caviar," Satoshi said. "I bet it would be terrible for their stomachs."

"Did you know that hot dogs are named after dachshunds — not the other way around?" Midori said.

"My brother is going to call him 'hot dog' all the time," Charlie said gloomily. "He's going to hate him. Because he hates everything."

"Maybe not," Satoshi said. "He likes his own dog. Maybe he'll like yours too."

Charlie just shook his head.

"Michelle has a great dog," Midori told Charlie. "He's a boxer."

"We just got him," I said. "We're, uh . . . still getting used to him."

"That sounds ominous," said Satoshi. They all looked at me as if they knew there was a story there.

"Well," I said. "We've had a couple of . . . problems." I didn't mean to complain about Tombo. But before I knew it I was telling them the whole story, about him eating Dad's shoe and then later all the destruction he'd caused when we left him home alone. They laughed a bit about the shoe, but by the end Midori had her hands over her mouth and Arnold was shaking his head in disbelief.

"That is crazy," Satoshi said. "Your *couch*? Seriously?"

"Nobody tell my parents that story," Arnold said. "Seriously, or else James and I will never be allowed to get a dog."

"I hope my new dog doesn't do anything like that," Charlie said with a nervous look. "Mom hates buying new furniture."

"I'm sure he won't," I said, resting my chin on my hand. "I'm sure my dog is the craziest one in town. It's like he turns into Godzilla when we leave him alone. I don't know what we're going to do."

"Don't worry." Midori reached across the table

and patted my hand. "Chihiro had some separation anxiety when we first got her too."

"Separation anxiety," I echoed. That sounded very official and psychological. I liked the feeling of having a diagnosis for Tombo's problems.

"But now she's used to not having us around," Satoshi agreed, nodding. "Tombo will calm down eventually too."

I hoped they were right. I felt a lot better having them to talk to, especially when I realized that I'd managed to not look over at Rosie's table or even think about Rosie for most of the lunch hour.

But there was a big part of me still worried about Tombo. I had a sinking feeling that we had a lot more problems to deal with before he finally calmed down . . . if he ever did.

CHAPTER 11

Dad looked extra frazzled when he picked me up after school. He kept patting his handkerchief over his bald head and tugging on his tie. It was weird enough that he was still in his suit; that meant he hadn't had time to change at home before coming to get me, although he normally was there half an hour earlier. I got an uneasy feeling in my stomach when I saw his face.

"So, Tombo didn't have the greatest day," Dad said as I shut the car door behind me.

"Uh-oh," I said. "But he was in the crate! How could he get in trouble from there?"

"Well," Dad said, "when your mom went home at lunch, she found that he'd clawed up his dog bed and tipped over his water bowl, so he was standing in a soggy mess of fluff and shredded sheepskin."

"Oh!" I said. "Poor Tombo!"

"I know, it sounds miserable, but it gets worse,"

Dad said. He turned out of the parking lot and I saw Parker Green and his friends walking along the sidewalk toward Parker's house. Rosie's brother Danny was with them, and so was the new guy. Behind us, Rosie and Pippa were getting into Rosie's mom's car, where I could see Buttons jumping at the windows with excitement. But I was not going to care. I was concentrating fiercely on not caring at all.

"You know the towel we left over the crate?" Dad went on. "Well, Tombo managed to drag it through the bars and chew it to pieces. There was almost nothing left of it."

I stared at Dad. "He *ate* the towel?"

"Pretty much," Dad said.

"That sounds really bad for him," I said. "Couldn't he make himself sick that way? What if bits of towel get stuck in his stomach?"

"Your mom had the same thought. But she had to get back to the office for an appointment. So she let him out in the yard, dried off the cage, cleaned out the dog bed remains, and called me."

"What did you do?" I asked.

He sighed. "I canceled my last appointment of the day and came home to take Tombo to the vet."

"Oh, no!" I said. I was terrified now. My first thought was that this was my fault. We shouldn't have left him in the crate — I should have argued more. But the next minute I realized he could have eaten something that would make him sick anywhere in the house, no matter where we left him. "Is he OK?"

"He's all right, sweetheart, don't worry." Dad patted my knee. "A little freaked out, and he'll seem woozy when you see him because Dr. Lee sedated him a little so she could x-ray him. Luckily we got him there in time so they could make him throw it all up, and she said there aren't any big pieces left inside that might block his stomach. But it was very dangerous. We really need to figure out what to do to stop his anxious chewing."

I nearly started crying; I couldn't believe poor Tombo had been in so much trouble, and I hadn't even been there to hug him and tell him it would all be all right. Maybe my lucky scarf was out of power. I wasn't supposed to have terrible days when I was wearing it.

"Don't worry, Michelle," Dad said. "We'll come up with something."

"You promise?" I said. "We'll keep trying? You won't take him back to the shelter?"

Dad's eyebrows went up. "Not until we've tried everything else," he said. "We made a commitment to this dog, and I want to help him. Don't you?"

"Yes!" I said. "I really do!"

"There's a good dog inside Tombo," Dad said. "Most dogs need a little help to be good, especially if they've had a tough life, but they're worth it. I have faith in him."

"So he's not bad to the bone?" I said, sniffling a little. We pulled into our driveway.

Dad laughed. "I don't think so," he said. "I think almost all dogs have good hearts, if you treat them right and train them correctly." He looked thoughtful. "Maybe we can find him an obedience class. I bet that would help."

"I'd go with him!" I said. "And I'd practice all the time to make sure he learns it all."

"He'd love that," Dad said with a smile.

I dropped my backpack inside the front door and ran out to the backyard. Tombo was lying on the grass in the sunshine, looking sleepy. Deandre sat in a deck chair beside him, reading *A Midsummer Night's Dream* for his English class.

Tombo lifted his head and gave me a lopsided grin with his tongue lolling out. His butt wiggled a bit like he wanted to get up and wag his tail, but he was too tired.

I flung myself onto the grass beside him and put my arms around his neck. He licked my chin with his big slurpy tongue. His short, smooth brown fur brushed against my cheek.

"Poor Tombo," I said. "How are you feeling? Does your tummy hurt? Is it like that time I ate too much birthday cake at Kelly's party? I was so sick — I hope you don't feel that bad. Can you believe you've already had to go to the vet? Poor sad dog!"

"I think he's kind of loving the attention," Deandre teased, poking Tombo gently with his toe.

"Deandre, what are we going to do?" I asked. "I mean, even tomorrow — how can we leave him alone at all if he's going to do crazy, dangerous, destructive things?"

"We'll have to put him in his crate and make sure there's nothing he can reach from there," Deandre said. "What other choice do we have?"

The empty crate seemed like kind of a sad, uncomfortable place to leave Tombo, but I couldn't think of any other options either. I thought about leaving him shut into my room, but there were *way* too many things he could eat in there, starting with all my scarves. I also thought about pretending to be sick so I could stay home with him. Then I could avoid Rosie *and* any questions from Ms. Applebaum about goats. The more I thought about it, the better that idea sounded to me.

But then, miraculously, a solution came to us in a totally unexpected way.

The phone rang while I was setting the table for dinner. I tensed, holding a glass of apple juice frozen over the table. Maybe it was Rosie, finally calling to say she was sorry and could we be friends again. If it was . . . what would I say?

Before I could make myself move across the kitchen, Dad answered the phone. I stared at him while he listened and saw his eyes flicker to me. It was for me! It had to be Rosie!

"Sure, hang on," Dad said. He held the phone out to me. "Someone called Midori?" he whispered.

I let out all my breath in a whoosh. I couldn't decide if I was disappointed or relieved. I wanted Rosie to reach out to me, but it would certainly be much easier and less stressful to talk to Midori than Rosie right now.

"Hey Midori!" I said, taking the phone into the den. I saw the wrecked couch and winced. Mom was hoping their warranty would help save it, but Dad was skeptical. I carried the phone into the living room instead and lay down on the long brown corduroy sofa in there.

A moment later, Tombo came trotting in after me and stuck his nose in my face, snuffling loudly. I reached over and rubbed his head.

"Hey!" Midori said. "I'm sorry about calling you — were you guys in the middle of dinner or anything?"

"Not yet," I said, "and whatever, you can call me anytime." Tombo nudged my hand so I could scratch behind his ears. He tried to wedge his nose under my head, but I scooted away from him — no way was he getting his jaws on my lucky scarf!

"Anytime?" she said. "Like three a.m.?"

"Uh," I said, "well, no, probably —"

Midori laughed. "I'm just kidding. My parents are kind of strict about when we can take phone calls, so I always check, just in case. Hey, listen, I realized I forgot to tell you something about tomorrow."

"Yeah?" I hoped she wasn't backing out. I really wanted to see Tombo and Chihiro play together some more. Besides, it would distract me from thinking about Rosie and Pippa hanging out and talking about me and having fun without me.

"It's just that, if you want Chihiro to come with me, we'll have to pick her up from day care. Is that OK?"

"Day care?" I said. "You mean, with lots of little kids? What?"

She laughed again. "No, it's a day care just for dogs. They watch her and take her out during the day while we're at work and school. She loves it — she gets to play with other dogs and she doesn't have to be alone all day."

I sat up so fast my head went dizzy for a minute. "That sounds perfect!" I cried. Tombo stood up on his hind legs and pawed the air, trying to share whatever I was so excited about. "Do they take other dogs? Will they take Tombo?"

"Rroof!" Tombo added, hearing his name.

"Uh . . ." Midori said. "They might. I can give you the phone number if you like."

"Yes, please!" I said. While she was looking for it, I told her about Tombo's terrible behavior with the towel and his visit to the vet.

"Aw, sad!" she said. "That won't happen at Bark

and Ride. They're great about watching the dogs and taking care of them."

I found a notepad and scribbled "Bark and Ride" on it, followed by the phone number as Midori read it off to me. Tombo stood beside me with his butt wagging as I wrote. When I put the pen down, he tried to snag the notepad in his mouth, right off the coffee table. I grabbed it and lifted it out of his reach, and then I had to dive for the pen as well. Tombo gave me a disgruntled look, like he couldn't believe how I kept thwarting him.

"Thanks so much, Midori," I said. "I'll tell my parents. And I'm sure it's no problem to pick up Chihiro from there tomorrow."

"Great!" she said. "OK, see you then!"

I hung up and patted Tombo's head. "This could be it, Tombo! Don't you think you'll be so happy at Bark and Ride?"

He looked from my face to the notepad and licked his chops, as if eating a pad of paper and a pen were the things that would *really* make him happy, and if I *cared* about him, I'd let him *have* them.

"Tombo, you're a goof," I said. "How can you possibly want to eat anything after your vet adventure today? I mean, seriously."

His head tilted to the left, then to the right, and then he made a mournful "Arroooo?" noise as if he was saying *But I'm HUNGRY*.

"So eat your kibble!" I said. "Not towels and shoes and pens! Good grief, Tombo."

Tombo sighed like I was too hopeless for words and trotted off to the kitchen.

I ran to tell my parents about the dog day care. I never knew there was such a thing. But it sounded like exactly what Tombo needed. Now we just had to hope they would take him!

CHAPTER 12

Alicia at Bark and Ride Day Care told us to stop by early in the morning for an evaluation, so Dad and I took Tombo over there half an hour before school. It turned out to be the cutest place, with rainbow paw prints on the walls and lots of toys and room for the dogs to play together. Tombo was already twitching with excitement as we walked in, because he could hear dogs yapping and running around in the main room. His ears flopped forward and his face had that wrinkly, determined, ready-to-scout-ahead look.

I liked how Alicia acted with Tombo too. She admired how handsome he was and let him sniff her hands, and then she brought out her own dogs to see how he'd react with them. I was pretty sure he'd be good, but it was a relief to see how funny and harmless and thrilled he was. He kept doing his little bow and rolling onto his back, and he stayed still while the little black one sniffed him intently.

Alicia said he seemed like a good dog, and she'd be willing to give him a trial for the day, especially since the Takashis had vouched for him. I thought that was really nice of Midori and her family, considering they didn't know Tombo that well. We also warned Alicia about his chewing problems and separation anxiety, and she said she'd seen plenty of that kind of thing.

"Usually being around all the other dogs is stimulating enough to prevent that behavior," she said. "Fingers crossed! We'll call you if there are any problems."

I saw Midori and her family pull up as we were leaving, and we waved at each other. Chihiro's sleek gray head poked out of a back window, her ears flapping in the breeze. I hoped Tombo would be happy to see her. More than that, I hoped he'd be good so the day care would let him come back!

Unfortunately, not all my problems could be left at a day care. The minute I walked into class, Ms. Applebaum called me over to her desk.

"Hey Michelle," she said. "Are you excited about raking leaves this weekend?"

I'd nearly forgotten about that part of the "Make a Difference" plan. We'd all been assigned to ask our family and friends if they knew anyone who wanted their lawn raked for twenty dollars, and we'd put up signs around town so other people could ask for us too. We already had ten houses signed up, including my grandparents'. That was two hundred dollars! I thought that had to be enough to buy a goat, especially with the bake sale money as well.

"Oh, yeah," I said. "That'll be fun." Except I knew what she was going to say next.

"Have you figured out how we're going to donate the goat?" Ms. Applebaum asked. "I think there's more than one charity that will do that . . . do you know which one you want to use? Or how much it'll cost?"

"Um," I said, poking the floor tiles with my sneaker. "I'm still working on that."

"All right," she said with a smile. "Let me know if you need help, OK?"

I nodded and hurried back to my desk. I wished I'd thought through this idea a bit more before suggesting it.

Rosie was at her desk with her nose in a book, ignoring me in a really obvious way. I tried not to look at her. Out of the corner of my eye, I could see Pippa glancing at us both nervously.

Ms. Applebaum stood up, tapping her ruler against her desk to make us be quiet.

"It's time to sign up for leaf-raking this weekend," she said. "Right now it looks like we can have two or three of you to a house, so I've printed up a list and I'll post it on the bulletin board. There are stars next to the bigger lawns, so if three of you want to rake together, please choose one of those houses. Try to sign up before the end of the day today, but if you need to talk to your parents first, let me know and you can sign up tomorrow."

I drew a spiral in the corner of my notebook, circling out from the center until it bumped into the edges. My pen felt wobbly in my hand. Rosie and Pippa and I had been planning to rake together. We'd talked about it last week, before Tombo arrived. Rosie's dad was planning to bake cookies and my mom would make sandwiches for us and we'd jump into leaf piles together and then go inside for cider and doughnuts with my grandparents when we were done.

But we couldn't do that if we weren't speaking to each other. Would we be friends again by Saturday? It was only Tuesday; maybe Rosie would say she was sorry in the next four days. But we had to sign up now. It was like Ms. Applebaum was making us decide about the future of our friendship before we were ready. I didn't know what to do.

I thought about it all morning, which made it kind of hard to concentrate on pilgrims or state capitals. By lunchtime, I was almost ready to go apologize to Rosie. Maybe if I just sat down next to her, she'd admit she was wrong and we could start over. We couldn't keep fighting like this forever, after all.

Maybe it wasn't worth it to win this fight, if it meant missing out on our plans together, or raking leaves by myself.

The bell rang, and we all got up to go to the cafeteria. Rosie marched over to the sign-up list and pulled out one of her pink pens with the feathers on the end. She wrote something on the sheet with a dramatic swish, and then turned and pulled Pippa out of the classroom. Pippa glanced back at me with a worried/sorry face.

A few other kids were crowded around the sheet now, but I went over and got close enough to see what Rosie had written.

She'd picked a house without a star next to it — a two-person house. And she'd written her name and Pippa's on the line beside it.

I scowled at the list. Well, that was just fine. I'd been prepared to be nice, but clearly she wasn't interested in being friends. I'd find someone else who liked cider and leaf-pile jumping.

My grandparents' house had a star, which I'd expected because their lawn is pretty big. I wrote my name on the line next to it, just to make sure no one else took it. "Michelle Matiba" looked kind of lonely there by itself.

I followed the rest of the class to the cafeteria, hoping Midori would want to rake leaves with me. But we'd need a third person, and most of the girls in class already had best friends. Who could we ask? One of the twins, Emmy or Kerri? I could barely tell the difference between them, and if we asked one the other would be mad at us.

Still, I didn't want to give Rosie the satisfaction of seeing that she'd upset me. So I took my tray with my gravy-covered turkey and wobbly orange Jell-O and marched right past her to Midori's table again. The boys still looked surprised to see me, but Midori scooted right over so I could sit next to her.

"I hope Tombo is having fun at Bark and Ride," Midori said, smiling at me.

"Me too!" I said. "He gave me such a funny look

when we left, like, hey, where are you guys going? You'll miss out! All the fun is here!" I tucked my hair scarf out of the way so I wouldn't get gravy on it. Today I was wearing one with a diamond pattern in black and green and red and yellow. The red matched my fleece, the dark green matched my shirt underneath, and the yellow matched my backpack.

"Are we all going to fit in your mom's car?" Midori asked. "Chihiro, Tombo, you, me, and Satoshi?"

I blinked for a minute. I hadn't realized that Satoshi was coming over to my house too. I tried to remember what we'd talked about and if that had come up. But I couldn't exactly *un*invite him.

"Yeah, sure," I said. "We'll squish in." Then I realized who our third leaf-raking person could be — maybe had to be, if they always did everything together. "Hey," I said, "do you and Satoshi want to rake with me on Saturday? I signed up for my grandparents' house, so if you join me, they'll give us cider and doughnuts after we're done. And I bet we could bring the dogs, as long as they mostly stay in the yard . . . Grandma and Grandpa have a kind of cluttered house."

"Doughnuts!" Satoshi said from across the table. "I'm in!"

"What?" Arnold said, perking up. "Doughnuts? Who's got doughnuts?"

"That sounds awesome," Midori said to me. "We'll check with our parents tonight, but it should be OK. As long as we're home in time to clean the house for my grandparents' big anniversary dinner on Sunday."

Satoshi groaned and put his head on the table. "Every relative in the universe is coming," he said. "We'll have to be polite *all day.*"

"At least Ray and Kai will be there," Midori pointed out. "Our cousins are visiting all the way from Japan," she explained to me. "They're really cool. And Chihiro loves them. I don't know what you're complaining about, Satoshi. You'll be in charge of playing with the cousins and the dog outside, so her fur doesn't bother Aunt Lisa's allergies. *I'll* have to make noodles and play the cello for Mee-maw and Paw-paw."

"Your fault for being a prodigy," he said, lifting his head up again with a teasing expression.

I liked the way Midori and Satoshi got along with each other. It reminded me of me and Deandre. Rosie always acted like it was *so* weird that I didn't hate my brother. She fights with all her brothers all the time, so she can't understand how Deandre and I don't fight that way too. But clearly we weren't so weird, if the Takashi twins could also be nice to each other.

When we got to Bark and Ride after school, I was as nervous as I felt the day of the spelling bee or before my chorus solo. It was like Tombo and I were being judged — Alicia even had some of the same facial expressions as Simon Cowell on *American Idol*. I really, really hoped Tombo had been good.

Alicia was smiling when we walked in the door.

"Well, your two dogs are certainly soul mates," she said. "We decided to let them share a cage during naptime — they didn't want to be parted from each other!"

"Awww," Midori and I said at the same time. Satoshi rolled his eyes, but he was smiling too.

"How was Tombo?" Mom asked Alicia.

"Did he fit in?" I asked. "Was he shy? Did he miss us? Did he mesh well with the established dynamics of the other dogs?"

"He was terrific," she said. "Lots of energy and lots of love. He wanted to be with us all day long; you just have to look at him and he comes running over to say hi and lick your hands. He did chew up a few of our toys during naptime, but we're used to that.

Tomorrow we'll make sure he gets the more inde-structible ones instead."

Tomorrow! I thought, overwhelmed with relief. *He can come back!*

Alicia sent one of the other employees to get Chihiro and Tombo for us, while we watched through the big window in her office. We could see Chihiro lying on a big stretchy dog bed in a corner, licking her paws. Tombo was racing around with a tiny golden Pomeranian.

The little dog had a stuffed football in its mouth, which Tombo kept trying to grab. But every time he lunged for it, the Pomeranian nimbly dodged or spun around and ran between Tombo's legs, so the boxer would end up standing there with a goofy expression, peering down at his paws, all *Where'd she go? Where'd she go?* Then the Pomeranian came running back and pretty much waved the football in Tombo's face as if she was taunting him, before she turned around to run off again with him right behind her.

I laughed. "Look at that!" I said to Midori. "I *knew* he could play well with little dogs. He would have loved Buttons, and I bet she'd have loved him too, if Rosie had just given them a chance."

Midori and Satoshi exchanged glances. "Is that what you guys are fighting about?" Satoshi asked.

I looked around to make sure my mom wasn't listening, but she was over by a rack of pamphlets, reading about obedience classes. I wasn't ready to have a full therapy session with my mom about my failing friendship with Rosie and how I'd handled it all wrong.

"Sort of," I said. "That and a bunch of other stuff. Whatever, it's all her fault, anyway. I'm waiting for her to apologize."

"Do you guys fight very often?" Satoshi asked casually.

Midori made a face at him. "Don't be nosy," she said.

"Oh, yeah, all the time," I said, trying to sound like I wasn't bothered by it. "It's no big deal."

Alicia's assistant led Tombo through the door, and the dog's whole body lit up when he saw us. His eyes went bright and his mouth dropped open into a huge smile and he flung himself to the end of his leash, straining to get to me. I ran over and hugged him and he slurped his tongue up my cheek.

"Good boy, Tombo!" I said. "You were so good! Good boy!"

Chihiro wriggled and bounced up and down behind him, waiting for her turn to get some attention. I leaned over and patted her head as Satoshi took her leash and Midori rubbed her sides.

"Did you show Tombo around?" Midori asked Chihiro. "Were you welcoming and friendly?"

"She was," Alicia assured us. "She stayed close to him all day. Even when he played with other dogs, he kept coming back to her. Although he's pretty fond of our Newfoundland, Yeti, too."

"That's Heidi Tyler's dog," Satoshi told me. He pointed through the window. "Look, you can see him in there."

I realized that Yeti was the huge black-and-white shaggy dog I'd seen in the park the other day. He was romping around the big playroom trying to get a small silky cocker spaniel puppy to play with him.

"Thank you so much," Mom said, shaking Alicia's hand.

"Yes, thank you!" I said. "And thank *you*, Midori, for telling us about this place."

"See you tomorrow, Tombo!" Alicia said, and he wagged his stumpy tail at her.

We all crammed into my mom's car with the dogs piled on top of the twins in the back. They didn't seem to mind — Midori burst out giggling every time Tombo climbed on her, which happened at least seven times on the way home.

Of course Mom had to bombard them with all kinds of embarrassing questions. "So you play the cello?" she said to Midori. "How long have you been doing that? How often do you practice? Do you enjoy it? That's very impressive. We tried to get Michelle to learn the flute a few years ago, but she couldn't stand all the practicing. What about you, Satoshi? What are you interested in? And tell me about your parents. What do they do?"

"*Mom*," I said. "Leave them alone for one second, can you?"

"I'm just curious," she said.

"It's OK," Satoshi said, but I was relieved when we finally got back to my house and could run out to the yard. I thought Tombo might leap right out of his fur, he was jumping around so much with excitement.

"This is great!" Midori said, unclipping Chihiro's leash. She stared around at our wide grassy lawn. "Look at all the space you have!"

"Race you to the other end!" Satoshi said to the dogs. He took off running and they both sprinted after him. Chihiro won by a mile, but mostly that was because Tombo got distracted halfway there and stopped to attack some falling leaves.

"I wish we could throw a tennis ball for him," I said to Midori. "But he eats them, like, faster than I can eat a bowl of peach sorbet. Which is my favorite, if you're wondering."

"You could try a Frisbee," she suggested. "And Furry Tails has some really tough toys and balls you could throw for him."

I was about to say that if we went back there, we'd have to leave Tombo at home after his behavior last time — but then I was struck by a terrible thought.

"Uh-oh," I said slowly. "Hey, Midori, the day care isn't open at night, too, is it?"

She shook her head. "Just seven a.m. to seven p.m., Monday through Friday."

"What are we going to do the rest of the time?" I said. "Like if we want to go out for dinner? Or over to my grandparents' house? Or even to the store on the weekend? How can we ever leave him alone, even for a little while?" I shook my head. "I'll always be worried that he's destroying something or hurting himself."

I'd been so excited about the day care — but really it could only solve half our problems with Tombo. The rest of the time, we were still on our own.

"Actually," Midori said. "I have an idea."

CHAPTER 13

I wasn't sure whether to say anything," Midori said. "Some people don't like it when you give them advice about their dogs."

Yeah. Like Rosie, I thought. The week before, I had told her about a video I saw on YouTube where a puppy learned to spin in circles, and she got all huffy and said she wasn't about to teach Buttons any tricks that made her dizzy.

"You can tell me anything," I said to Midori. "We'll take all the advice we can get!"

She went and got her messenger bag from the kitchen, where we'd left our stuff. She sat down on the back steps and I sat beside her. Chihiro and Tombo were wrestling playfully in the grass, pouncing on each other's shoulders and trying to be the dog on top. It was funny to see Tombo act like a boxer, getting up on his back paws and trying to bat at Chihiro with his front paws.

Satoshi came jogging back toward us when he saw us sitting down.

"You're going to give it to her?" he asked his sister as he flopped down on the grass next to us.

Midori nodded. She pulled a big, funny-looking bone out of her bag. It wasn't a real bone, but it was shaped like the ones you see in cartoons, long with a big knot on each end. It was a pale sand-white all over. She handed it to me. It felt dry and solid and a little crackly like really thick paper under my fingers.

"This is rawhide," Midori said. "You can get it in lots of different shapes and sizes; this is one of the big ones. Most dogs love it — they'll chew on it for hours, and it's really good for their teeth."

I turned it over and squeezed it. It felt pretty hard; I didn't think *my* teeth would make much of a dent in it! But of course Tombo's were much bigger than mine.

"So if we give this to Tombo, he'll chew on this instead of ripping up other things?" I asked.

"Hopefully!" said Midori. "It'll help if he's tired and well-exercised, too, but we leave one of these in Chihiro's crate with her and it keeps her busy for hours. She barely even notices we're gone."

"Wow!" I said.

"Want to test it out?" Satoshi suggested. "We'll put him in his crate with this and then leave for a few minutes and see what happens."

"We can watch him through the back window!" I said. "Let's try it!"

Of course, convincing Tombo to abandon his game with Chihiro took a while. When I called him, he looked over at me like, *Um, hello, can't you see I'm in the middle of a very important wrestling move right here?* The big gray dog had him pinned under her front paws and was chomping playfully on his head. This was apparently everything Tombo had ever wanted out of life, judging by the dopey expression of glee on his face.

Midori called Chihiro, and immediately the Weimaraner ran over and sat politely in front of her. Satoshi saw my face and hid a smile. "I'm sure Tombo will be good at that soon," he reassured me.

"Hmmm," I said. "I'll believe it when I see it." Abandoned by his playmate, Tombo was rolling on his back in the grass with all his paws flapping in the air.

"Come on, Tombo," I called. He wriggled upright and galloped over to us. I held the rawhide bone out so he could sniff it. Immediately he tried to grab it in his jaws. I pulled it back out of reach and beckoned him into the house.

Mom was in the kitchen reading a book and stirring a pot of soup at the same time. She squinted at me as Tombo and I came in.

"Are they done playing already?"

"No," I said, "but we're going to test out a way to leave him in his crate. You know, in case we want to go out at night. Check this out!" I held out the bone to her.

"Oh, rawhide bones," she said. "That's a good idea."

"Midori thought of it," I said. "OK, Tombo, go to your room!" I pointed at the crate. Tombo wrinkled his forehead skeptically. I waved the bone in front of the open door. "Go to your room and you get this!"

Tombo kind of snort-sighed and leaned forward, as if he was hoping he could just take the bone, but I held it farther into the cage. Hesitantly, he stepped inside, and I let him take the bone in his mouth. Then I shut the door behind him and stood back.

Tombo circled for a minute on the newspapers my mom had left at the bottom of the crate. The bone stuck out of his mouth goofily, like one of my grandpa's cigars. Finally he lay down, propped the bone up between his front paws, and started going to town on one end of it. His eyes half-closed and his teeth went *chomp chomp chew chew chomp chomp chomp*.

"He loves it!" I said. "Come on outside and let's see if he notices he's alone."

Mom put down her book and followed me out the back door. Midori and Satoshi were already standing at the back window peering in through the glass.

"He didn't look up when you closed the door," Midori whispered.

"He's still chewing," Satoshi added.

Chihiro wagged her tail at us like, *This is a weird game, huh? Where's my friend gone?*

I cupped my hands around my eyes and peeked in. Mom did the same thing beside me.

Sure enough, Tombo was slurping away in the same position we'd left him in. He kept tilting his head one way and then the other, gnawing on the bone with his back teeth.

"Yay!" I whispered. "Look at that! Totally better than chewing shoes!"

"Or eating towels," Mom agreed.

We watched for a few more minutes, but he just kept chewing happily. "I think this might work!" I said to Midori. "I can't believe it. I guess he's not really 'bad to the bone,' right, Mom?"

"I never thought he was," she said.

"Except that he's bad to the *bone*," I said, pointing at the rawhide. "Ha-ha! Get it? Because he's chewing up the bone?"

Satoshi groaned and Midori pretended to slap her forehead. "I cannot believe you just said that," she said. "That was such a Charlie kind of joke." But she was giggling, and Mom hid a smile too.

"Well, I'm just glad there's something that'll make him be good," I said.

"And if he gets bored with rawhide," Midori said, "there are all these other things you can give him to chew. Like, there are toys you stuff with treats or peanut butter — Chihiro will spend forever trying to get the treats out. Or there are real chunks of cow bones and stuff you can get at the pet store."

"Gross!" I said.

"But if it makes him happy . . ." Mom said with a shrug.

"OK, I think that's enough of a test," I said. "Let's bring him back out so he can play with Chihiro some more."

When I opened the back door, Tombo glanced

sideways at me and blinked a little like, *Oh, hey, it's you. Did you go somewhere?* I opened his crate and he stayed where he was, *yarm yarm yarm*ing on his bone. I had to get another treat to distract him and lure him out, and then we hid the bone so we could use it only when we had to go out.

Luckily Tombo didn't seem to have a very long memory. By the time the bone was hidden, he was all ready to go outside and run around again.

"Dogs are funny," I said to Mom as I opened the back door for him. We watched him sprint across the grass with Chihiro leaping on his back and the Takashi twins chasing them. "The ways to solve their problems are so logical and simple, once you figure them out."

"If only people were like that," Mom said, shaking her head.

No kidding, I thought. Wouldn't everything be great if I could just give Rosie a bone to make her stop bossing people around? Or if I could distract her from Pippa with a treat as easily as I distracted Tombo from his rawhide?

Unfortunately, I knew it wasn't going to be that easy . . . and the truth was, I had no idea if Rosie and I would ever be able to be friends again.

CHAPTER 14

I took Midori upstairs to show her my room before they went home. Unlike Rosie, she thought it was really cool, and she didn't say anything about how messy or mismatched it was. She loved the photos of Africa and she went crazy for my rainbow waterfall of scarves on the coatrack.

"They're all so beautiful!" she said. "How do you decide which one to wear each day? I never see you wear the same one twice in a row."

"I have a system for that," I said. "Once I wear it, I move it to the bottom hooks of the coatrack. Then I gradually move the scarves up as I go through them, so by the time it gets to the top again, I know it's been a while since I wore it."

Midori looked impressed. "That's very organized of you."

"That might be the only way I'm organized!" I said with a laugh.

She gently touched the scarves on the top hooks. "So you'll wear one of these tomorrow?"

"Yeah, this one, I think," I said, lifting off a midnight-blue scarf with flecks of silver thread like stars in a night sky and silver braided tassels on the ends.

"That is gorgeous," said Midori, feeling the smooth satin. "I've always loved the scarves you wear."

"I get new ones from my Kenyan side of the family every Christmas," I said. "I think they first chose them because they're lighter to mail than other presents. And then other people started getting them for me, too, and it kind of became my thing."

"How many do you have?" she asked.

"Eighty-four," I said proudly. "I bet I can get to a hundred by the end of elementary school." It was nice to have a friend who thought that was as cool as I did.

After the twins left, I went onto my dad's computer and tried to figure out the goat charity research I'd promised Ms. Applebaum I would do. Tombo flopped down on the floor underneath me and started snoring about five seconds later. Day care and playing with Chihiro had really worn him out. I rested my bare feet on his solid brown torso and he just made a snortling noise in his sleep.

I went to Google and typed in "goat," but that only got me lots of information about raising goats and types of goats. So then I typed in "goat Africa" instead, and got about three million results: give a goat for Christmas, buy a goat for Africa, donate a goat, something about goat meat that I definitely did not want to click on . . .

There was too much information! How was I supposed to choose which charity was best? How could I even tell which ones were real charities? What if I clicked on the wrong link and accidentally put a virus on my dad's computer? Mom and Dad are always warning me about going to strange websites. They are super-careful about everything to do with the Internet.

I sighed and Tombo woke up. He pushed himself into a sitting position and looked at me. His forehead was all wrinkled in that cute worried way again. It was as if he knew how stressed out I was and he was wishing he could help.

"It's too confusing, Tombo," I said.

He tilted his head. He looked like he was listening as hard as he could.

"Any advice?" I asked him. "How would you send a goat to Africa?"

He thought about that for a long moment, then tilted his head the other way. It made his ears flop over adorably, but it wasn't very helpful.

"Oh, well," I said. "I'll deal with it later."

Tombo liked that plan. He rested his chin on my knee while I closed the Internet window and turned off the computer. His big brown eyes looked up at me reassuringly.

"I can tell you one person I'm not going to ask for advice," I said to him. "And that's Rosie. She'd probably send *you* to Africa if she could."

Tombo's butt wiggled a little, so I guess he wasn't listening all that carefully.

After dinner, Dad and Deandre and I took Tombo for a long walk to make sure he was really, *really* tired, so he wouldn't eat or chew anything overnight. It worked on me, too — I was so tired by the time I got into bed that I didn't even have time to worry about Rosie or goats before I fell fast asleep.

It wasn't until I woke up on Wednesday morning that I remembered to worry about what I would do after school that day. Mom and Dad wouldn't be home until five, and I couldn't go to Rosie's mom's store with her and Pippa the way I usually did. But it was a bit late to tell Mom and Dad that. They didn't even know that Rosie and I were fighting.

At school, I kept sneaking glances at Rosie all morning. *Maybe I should just go over and sit down with her at lunch.* Maybe if I pretended like nothing had happened, we could start acting like we were friends again, and then I could hang out with them after school and there wouldn't be anything to worry about.

Halfway through our math lesson, Rosie got up to sharpen her pencil at the pencil sharpener beside the bulletin board. I saw her glance up at the leaf-raking sign-up sheet, where Midori had written her name and Satoshi's next to mine. Rosie narrowed her eyes at the list, then looked over her shoulder to glare at Midori. Luckily Midori had her head down, taking notes, and didn't see the way Rosie was looking at her.

But it turned out somebody else noticed.

As we were lining up for lunch, Satoshi tapped my shoulder and said in a low voice, "Can I talk to you?"

I was about to say yes when Rosie came sweeping

up with Pippa right behind her. She raised an eyebrow at Satoshi and tossed her hair.

"Oh, *excuse* me," she said. "Am I *interrupting* anything?" Her voice sounded like it was loaded with extra meaning.

"No," I said, putting my hands on my hips.

"Well." Rosie angled her shoulder to shut Satoshi out of our conversation. "I just wanted to tell you, Michelle, that my mom got in that order of silk scarves you helped pick out of the catalog last month. Remember?"

I did remember. Mrs. Sanchez had found an amazing artist who hand-painted silk scarves, and she had said if I helped her choose which ones to order for her shop, she'd let me have one at a discount. I'd seen one with a pattern like yellow autumn leaves reflected in water, with gray river stones underneath. It was beautiful, and I'd been dreaming of it ever since.

"Sooooooo," Rosie said, "if you want to come to the store with us after school and get your scarf, I'll let you sit with us at lunch today."

Behind her back, I saw Satoshi make a face like, *That's nice of you, Your Highness.*

"Really?" I said. "Because I was thinking —"

"And all you have to do," Rosie interrupted, "is say you're sorry for all the mean things you said to me on Sunday."

"Me?" I said. "What about the mean things *you* said? Especially about Tombo?"

"Everything I said was true," Rosie pointed out. "He *is* big. I mean, you can't argue with that."

"But he's a good dog," I said, faltering. Maybe it was stupid to keep fighting. I really wanted that scarf . . . and more than that, I wanted my friends back. Didn't I?

"Think about it," Rosie said, glancing at her watch. "You have two minutes until we get to the cafeteria." She took Pippa's arm and dragged her to the front of the line.

Satoshi had his face set in a careful expression, like he didn't want me to know what he was thinking. "Rosie's very . . . direct," he said.

"That's one of the things I liked about her," I said. "She always says what she's thinking. There's not a lot of mystery and weirdness. If she likes you, you'll know."

"Yeah," he said. "Same if she doesn't."

"And if she's mad at you, you know right away,"

I said. "Instead of having to guess for weeks and trying to figure out what's wrong or if it's not even anything to do with you. My best friend before her was like that." That was in first grade, before we moved here. Because of Kelly, my mom had to explain the phrase "passive-aggressive" to me when I was seven, although I still wasn't sure I understood it.

Satoshi shrugged. "I guess I'd rather have a friend who doesn't get mad at me at all."

I was about to say, "But nobody's that perfect," when I realized that Pippa never seemed to get mad at anyone. Even when Rosie was really bossy with her, Pippa stayed sweet. And I imagined that Charlie never got mad at Satoshi, either; I couldn't imagine him ever yelling at anyone. It probably wasn't healthy to never express your anger like that, though. My parents would say that repressing your emotions only makes them build up more.

"Listen," Satoshi said as the line started to move toward the cafeteria. I glanced back and saw Midori a few people behind us, talking to Charlie. It didn't look like she'd heard any of the Rosie conversation; she was talking really fast and waving her hands in a way that made me guess she was telling him about Chihiro and Tombo playing together.

"I just want to check," Satoshi said. "I mean — not to be weird or anything — but I just want to make sure that you really want to be friends with Midori."

I looked at him in surprise. "Of course I do!" I said. "Midori is awesome."

"*I* know that," he said. "But I mean, if you're only being friends with her until Rosie takes you back . . . that wouldn't be very cool. Because she wants to stay friends with you. So, I guess I was just wondering if this is only temporary, or what."

I made myself stop and think about what he'd said. To be honest, there was a part of me that expected to end up back at Rosie's lunch table, seeing Rosie and Pippa almost every day after school. I mean, it's not like I planned to ditch Midori or anything. It's just that Rosie had been my best friend for so long, I kind of thought it would always be that way, once we were done fighting.

But would that be mean to Midori? I had never even thought of that.

Well, now I was officially confused. Midori had been really great to me, and I loved her dog. But how could I tell after two days whether she ought to replace my best friend of three years?

"Besides," Satoshi said, "I'm worried Rosie might stay mad at Midori, even if you go back to being friends. I get the feeling she doesn't like competing for things." We'd reached the cafeteria and he followed me to the line for grilled chicken sandwiches.

"No, she loves competing," I said. "It's losing she doesn't like."

He laughed a little. "Well, anyway," he said. "I just wanted to make sure you'd thought about it. But you should do whatever you want, of course." He nodded and ducked out of the line, heading for his table.

I stood there for a long time, staring at the apples and pears and Jell-O, trying to decide what to do. I mean, not about whether to have an apple or a pear, although that's probably what it looked like.

Should I go sit with Rosie, say I was sorry, and go on with my life as normal? That would mean Wednesdays at her mom's store, the scarf that was waiting for me, playing with Buttons, and knowing where I belonged. But it also probably meant the same problems with Pippa as before. If anything, Rosie might leave me out even more now that we'd fought about it. Not only that, but she'd made it clear what she thought of my dog, so that would always be a problem. If she never apologized, how would I ever stop being mad at her?

And how could she not like poor Tombo? It wasn't fair.

So maybe I should sit with Midori. She liked Tombo, and it was just as much fun playing with Tombo and Chihiro as it was playing with Buttons. Plus Midori had been really helpful with our Tombo problems so far. And I knew we liked the same movies, at least.

But what else did I know about her? I'd have to learn the important best friend things all over again, like all her favorite clothes — I didn't even know her favorite color! What would it be like to have her as a best friend instead of Rosie? What if there was something about her that I didn't know?

Mom and Dad were always finding surprising things wrong with their patients. You couldn't tell people were crazy just by looking at them. What if Midori spent every weekend studying really hard and I'd have no one to hang out with? Or what if she suddenly decided to skip sixth grade, so I'd be left alone next year?

Then again . . . what if she was just a better friend than Rosie?

Well, I couldn't stand there avoiding the decision for the rest of lunch. I picked up a greenish-yellow pear, put it on my tray, and moved on to the cashier. Then I flipped the ends of my blue scarf back over my shoulders, lifted my tray, and marched across the cafeteria — right past Rosie to Midori's table.

CHAPTER 15

Satoshi looked really happy when I scooted in beside him. Midori, across the table, was smiling as always.

"Hey, did you notice?" she asked me. She held out her arm, and I realized that she was wearing a midnight blue shirt the same color as my scarf. Her straight black hair was clipped back with shimmery silver barrettes that matched the tassels and starry threads.

"We match again!" she said with a grin. "Not so much by accident this time, though. I hope that's OK."

"I love it!" I said. Rosie laughed at me the one time I suggested matching our outfits, because pink was *her* color, so she didn't want everyone else to wear it and she definitely wasn't about to wear anything else. "What color are you going to wear tomorrow? I bet I can match anything you've got."

"Really?" she said. "How about — a lime green sweater with a hot pink turtleneck underneath?"

"Too easy," I said. "My watermelon scarf it is! But now you actually have to wear that."

"Wait, wait," she said, giggling. "Don't make me do that. How about peach? I have a new peach-colored sweater I could wear."

"No problem," I said. "I have a dark purple scarf with, like, a peach cloud pattern across it. It's hard to describe, but it's pretty."

"Cool," Midori said.

Satoshi shook his head. "Matching outfits. Girls are weird."

"Aw, are you feeling left out?" Midori teased. "You can wear peach tomorrow, too, if you want."

Satoshi made a face and changed the subject. "Are you going to finish your water?" he asked her.

"Yeah, but I can get another one," she said, jumping up. "Be right back."

While she was gone, Satoshi leaned over and said, "Don't look now, but I think there's actually smoke coming out of Rosie's ears."

I giggled, but there was a pit of nervousness in my stomach. I'd wanted to be brave and fearless and choose the person who seemed to deserve my friendship — and even though it was new, I really felt like that person was Midori.

But it still kind of scared me. Especially when I thought about the end of the school day and what I would do while Rosie and Pippa went off to the store. That's where my parents would think I was. What would I do instead? If only I could go to Tombo's day care and hang out with a bunch of dogs like he did.

"What are you doing after school today?" I asked Midori when she sat back down.

She made a face. "The entire family is going shopping for my grandparents' anniversary dinner. My mom has the whole menu planned out. We have to go to this Asian food market she likes that's forty-five minutes away. And then we have to find them a present from me and Satoshi."

"Should be really fun," Satoshi said glumly.

"We love Mee-maw and Paw-paw," Midori said, "but they keep saying they don't want presents. Except Mom is sure they don't mean it, so now what are we supposed to do?"

"For my grandpa's last birthday, Deandre and I got him a cookbook," I said. "And we gave

Grandma a framed photo of us with her. She really liked that."

"That could work," Satoshi said to Midori. "I bet there's a good photo on the digital camera — then all we'd need is a frame."

"And they'd have to like it, because it's not clutter, it's their grandchildren!" Midori said, grinning. "Yeah, maybe we should do that. Thanks, Michelle!"

"No problem," I said.

But *I* still had a problem . . . what was I going to do after school? I couldn't tag along with Midori and Satoshi. If only I'd told Mom and Dad about fighting with Rosie.

When the bell rang at the end of the day, I stood up and packed my things as slowly as I could. By the time I was finished, everyone else was gone except for Ms. Applebaum, who was wiping down the board. She turned around and smiled at me.

"So how's the project going?" she asked me. "Have you decided what we should do?"

I sighed. It was too hard to deal with Rosie and Tombo and the goat problem all at the same time. I had to tell her the truth.

"I can't figure it out," I blurted. "I tried looking online, but it seemed like there were so many charities and I didn't know which sites to click on or which ones to believe or how to tell which one was best. I think I need help."

"That's all right," said Ms. Applebaum. She didn't sound mad or disappointed at all. "We can figure it out together."

"Really?" I said. "Where do we start?"

"Where you did — online," she answered. "Is there a day you could stay a bit late after school to work on this?"

"Today!" I yelped. "I mean, today would be great, if that's OK with you."

"Sure. I like your spirit," she said with a smile.

I called and told Mom I'd be staying late at the school, and then Ms. Applebaum and I went down to the computer lab. She typed "goat Africa charity" into the search engine. A lot of what came up looked like the results I'd seen the night before.

"See?" I said. "There's, like, a million links."

Ms. Applebaum scanned the first page. "A lot of these are articles *about* donating goats, though," she said. "Only a few of these link directly to charities. And here's a link to a site that compares charities to tell you which ones are most effective. We can double-check that the charities are real there."

We read about goats and cows and sheep and chickens for about an hour. We found charities that paid for schools and books, and others that helped women start small businesses in their communities. There were some that used donations to fix medical problems or build hospitals, and others where the money bought mosquito nets that would save people from malaria.

With some organizations, you just gave the money and they figured out where it was most needed; with others, you could pick which project you liked. A lot of them were in the United Kingdom, so the costs were in pounds, which was a little confusing for me.

There were so many different ways to help. It was kind of overwhelming. It was like walking through the pet shelter — the same way I wanted to take all the dogs home, I wanted to give our bake sale money to all these charities so we could help people go to school and get healthy and live better lives.

Ms. Applebaum looked pleased when I told her that. "We can do more bake sales and other things too," she said. "I'd love for you guys to support more projects like this."

Finally we picked a charity we liked called Heifer International, where you can donate goats or geese or llamas or all kinds of things. It had good ratings and comments and an easy way to donate with a credit card online. Plus the picture of the goat on the website was really cute.

Ms. Applebaum said she would check with the principal about using a school credit card, so I didn't have to worry about that. And the amazing thing was that the goat was only a hundred and twenty dollars. We nearly had that much already, and that was before leaf raking! Maybe we could use the rest of the money to get something else, too, like a pig or a flock of ducks or a trio of rabbits.

I was so excited as Ms. Applebaum drove me home. My "Make a Difference" project was really going to happen. I wanted to write to Grandma in Kenya right away to tell her. I knew she'd be proud of me.

Not to mention it was a huge relief not to have the goat hanging over my head. I hadn't even realized how much I'd been worrying about it until I didn't have to anymore.

It made me feel a lot better about Rosie and Tombo too. Maybe I'd been worrying too much about them as well. Looking at all those charities made me feel like my problems weren't that big. At least I had shoes and could go to school and afford books and stuff. Plus I had a dog of my own to love no matter what problems I had with my friends.

Maybe all I needed was a little help, and everything would turn out all right.

CHAPTER 16

I realized something," I said to Midori.

She stopped raking for a moment and pushed her dark hair out of her eyes with the back of her wrist. It had been pulled back in a ponytail at first, but after an hour of raking, bits of it had fallen loose into her face. She kept taking off her gloves to try and fix it, but it just got messy again. I was glad for my autumn-colored scarf — matching the golden yellow turtleneck Midori was wearing — which kept all my hair neatly pulled away from my face, as always.

"What's that?" she asked.

Our class had lucked out with the weather for leaf-raking day. It was a beautiful Saturday, clear and crisp and sunny, with bright blue skies above us and tangerine orange and burgundy red leaves crunching below us. The air had that windy fall feeling where it's not too cold yet but there's a faraway feeling of snow and Christmas and cranberries and pumpkin pie on the way.

My grandparents had welcomed us first thing in the morning with hot chocolate (mine without milk) and freshly baked blueberry muffins. More delicious smells started wafting from Grandpa's kitchen as we got closer to lunchtime. I had a feeling we'd be getting much more than cider and doughnuts. Grandpa's face lit up into his happy "cooking for new people" look when he saw Satoshi and Midori.

"Well, I was thinking," I said, "about Tombo and the way he was chewing everything."

We looked over at Chihiro and Tombo, who were galloping around the yard together. Chihiro kept spinning away from him so Tombo would have to chase her, and then Tombo pounced on her head and tugged on her ears with his teeth. Then she'd whip around and knock him over and they rolled together in the grass, making playful growling and yipping sounds. Satoshi was trying to rake under the big maple tree, but they kept plowing into him by accident or scattering his leaf pile and then looking baffled when he chased them off.

"Tombo was so fixated on chewing stuff," I said.

"He really really wanted to chew on my dad's shoes or the leather couch, because he thought they were the best possible things in the world for him to chew on. But then you came along with the rawhide bone, and we got him that big disgusting cow bone yesterday, and now he loves them and doesn't want to chew anything else."

Midori nodded. "Sure, OK," she said.

"So I was being like Tombo," I said. "I was convinced that Rosie was the one person in the world I wanted to be best friends with. I didn't even think I had other choices, or that I'd want them. But then you came along, and now I know you're much cooler than her and I just want to be best friends with you instead."

For a moment, Midori looked pleased and a little embarrassed. Then a thought flitted across her face and she frowned. "Wait a minute," she said. "So, in this analogy, Rosie is a leather couch . . . and I'm a big disgusting cow bone?"

"Um," I said. "Hang on, that's not what I mean. I mean, I mean it in a good way!"

Midori burst out laughing. "Well, thanks," she said. "I think."

Tombo came bounding over to find out what we

were laughing about. He charged right through my pile of leaves — for about the tenth time that morning, I might add.

"Ack! Tombo! Quit that!" I yelped.

He stood up on his back paws and waved his front paws at me. I let him put his paws on my shoulders and gave him a hug. He wagged his butt happily and licked the side of my face from my neck to my hairline.

"Eeek," I squealed, rubbing my cheek. "Tombo, you're slobbery."

He licked me again, as if he was saying *I know, aren't I fabulous?*

"The only kind of sad thing," I said to Midori over Tombo's head, "is that I would have liked to play with Buttons more. She's pretty cute, even if she's not as big and goofy as our dogs."

"Well, you don't have to stop being friends with Rosie forever," Midori pointed out. "Maybe you just need a break from each other for a while. She'll see that she can't boss you around, and you find out you can have other friends besides her. Then later when you've both cooled off, you can be friends again."

"Maybe," I said. "One day. If there's something that makes us hang out again, I could maybe see that happening. But you're my best friend now. That's not going to change."

She ducked her head and smiled.

"So even if Rosie and I do become friends again," I said, "she'll have to put up with *two* big dogs coming to play, not just mine."

"That'd be fun. Chihiro likes little dogs," Midori assured me. "She's very gentle with them."

"ROARF!" Chihiro barked from across the yard. Tombo dropped to all fours and spun around to look at her. She did a play bow, wagging her tail slowly and giving him a *Come and get me* face.

Tombo glanced back at me.

"Go ahead and play, Tombo," I said to him, patting his head. "You deserve it. You know why?"

He wagged his butt like he knew what I was about to say.

"Because, as I suspected from the beginning, you're a good dog after all," I said, and he beamed like I'd just showered him with chew toys.

King is a great dog . . .
and a lot of trouble!

Pet Trouble
Dachshund Disaster

Turn the page for a sneak peek!

I was nervous as we rang the doorbell at the dog's foster house. The dachshund was really cute in the photo online, but what if he was weird in real life? What if he was hyper or boring or crazy? Or worse, what if he didn't like me at all?

Immediately there was a volley of loud, high-pitched barking from inside. It sounded like more than one dog. Mom rubbed her purse strap anxiously. "I hope that's not *our* new dog making all that noise," she joked.

We're not used to noisy dogs in our house. Bowser never barks at the doorbell or the mailman or people coming in. At most he'll stand at the top of the stairs and growl. He only barks sometimes at other dogs, like if he sees them across the street from our yard.

An old man in a pink plaid sweater vest opened the door and smiled at us. "You must be the Graysons," he said. "I'm Milton Schwartz — come in, come in."

"My name is Aidan," Aidan announced with a big smile as he stepped inside. "Nice to meet you, sir." He held out his hand for Milton to shake, so then of course I had to do that, too. Aidan can be a little weird and old-fashioned like that with grown-ups, but Milton seemed to like it.

"Ruthie, they're here!" he called. We could still hear barking from the back rooms.

"Uh — how many dogs do you have?" Mom asked.

"Seven at the moment," Milton said. "Three of our own and four that we're fostering until they find good homes. We just can't resist their little faces, and since our kids moved out, it sure keeps us busy." He grinned as his wife came into the room. She had silver hair pinned into a loose bun and a pink tracksuit that matched his sweater vest.

She was carrying the most handsome dog I'd ever seen.

"Oh!" Aidan cried, pressing his hands to his chest dramatically.

The dachshund had floppy brown ears and a long brown body with short fur and little stubby legs. His black eyes were shining and alert, darting from my mom to me to Aidan and back again.

"We've been calling him Chutzpah," Milton said. The way he said it sounded like "Hoots-pah." "Ruthie says it's very appropriate for such a bold, nosy little dog!"

I looked at Mom and she laughed politely, although I don't think she completely understood the joke either. It didn't matter, though; I would definitely be changing his name — just as soon as I thought of one that was perfect for him.

"Which of you is Charlie?" Ruth asked, smiling at us.

I waved, and she beckoned me over. We both knelt on the floor and she set the dog down between us. I held out my hand and he sniffed it really thoroughly with his long nose, starting at my fingertips and going down to my wrist and then back up my thumb.

"Here," Ruth whispered, passing me a dog treat. "These are his favorites."

I held out the treat and his tail swooshed up and started wagging. He looked up into my face and opened his mouth a bit like he was smiling.

"Sit," I said. I'd been watching *The Dog Whisperer* and *It's Me or the Dog* nonstop for a week, so I knew you were supposed to make the dog do something to earn its treat each time.

But the dog just kept looking at me, and Ruth and Milton both laughed. "Good luck with that!" Milton said. "We've been trying for a month and it's pretty much impossible to teach him anything."

"Impossible?" Mom said in a worried voice.

"Oh, but he's house-trained!" Ruth reassured her. "We figured that was the most important thing."

"Sure," Mom said. "Yes. True." She tucked a strand of red hair behind her ear and studied the dog.

The dachshund's tail was still wagging. His sharp black eyes were fixed on the treat now. I didn't know what else to do, so I just gave him the treat. His ears flapped as he chomped it down and then licked my fingers.

"Dachshunds are like that," Milton added. "Stubborn, but very cute."

"And very loyal," Ruth said. I liked the sound of that. I wanted my dog to be loyal to me more than anything.

The dachshund suddenly took a step forward and planted his front paws on my knees. He leaned up toward my face with his tail wagging.

"Wow," Milton said. "He likes you!"

"He's usually much more nervous around strangers," Ruth said admiringly.

I grinned at the dog. Slowly, so I wouldn't startle him, I reached out and stroked his smooth head and back. His tail wagged even harder. His fur was short and a little oily under my fingers. I felt like I could sit there and pet him forever.

"This looks like a match to me!" Ruth proclaimed.

Milton started talking to my mom about the paperwork while Ruthie went to get a bag of things for the dog. I scratched behind the dachshund's long, shiny ears. He pulled himself all the way into my lap and sat down.

"Can I say hi?" Aidan asked suddenly from behind me, and the dog and I both jumped. Without waiting for an answer, Aidan was already reaching for the dog's face. "Hi dog! Can I hug him, please, can I?"

"I don't think he'd like that," I said, trying to shift away from Aidan's grasping hands.

"I just want to hold him," Aidan said. He leaned around me and reached for the dog again.

Suddenly the dachshund went "RARF! RARF!" very loudly right in Aidan's face.

Startled, Aidan jumped back and fell over on his butt. The dog wriggled around in my arms, licked my neck, and looked back at Aidan like, *Yeah, and stay out!*

I was afraid Aidan would start crying, but I guess he was too surprised to cry. I mean, pretty much no one ever yells at him, and usually animals love him. I felt a little bad about the bewildered look on Aidan's face, but I also felt a terrific explosion of happiness inside me. The dog had chosen *me* over sweet, adorable Aidan. That *never* happened.

"Everything OK here?" Mom asked, coming back over to us.

"Yup," I said, rubbing the dog's head. "Everything's perfect."

I had no idea how wrong I was.

Read them all!

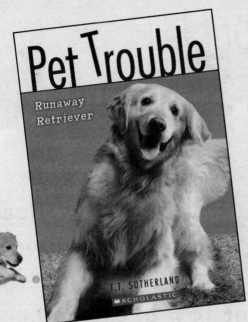

Runaway Retriever

Merlin is a great dog.

Parker's new golden retriever is a guy's best friend, with tons of energy for walks and playing catch. And Merlin clearly thinks Parker is the best thing since rawhide bones.

There's just one thing . . .

Merlin is an escape artist. No fence is too high, no cage too strong to keep him from following Parker everywhere he goes. Can Parker make Merlin sit—and *stay*?

Loudest Beagle on the Block

Trumpet is a great dog.

Ella spends all her time inside, practicing her music for the school talent show. But with her new beagle, Trumpet, she's starting to make new friends and see a whole world away from the piano bench.

There's just one thing . . .

Every time Ella starts to sing, Trumpet howls. Loudly. If Ella doesn't lose her canine costar, she doesn't stand a chance at the show—but can tone-deaf Trumpet tone it down?

Mud-Puddle Poodle

Buttons is a great dog.

When she finally gets a dog of her own, Rosie knows it's going to be perfect—unlike everything else in her chaotic house with four crazy brothers.

There's just one thing . . .

Buttons hates her fancy dog pillow, but she loves a good, dirty pile of leaves! Rosie's new pet is her complete opposite. Can she ever learn to live with this mess of a dog?

Bulldog Won't Budge

Meatball is a great dog.

Eric has always wanted a dog, so when a bulldog named Meatball is abandoned at his mother's veterinarian office, Eric is sure it's fate—he can give Meatball a new home!

There's just one thing . . .

Meatball is stubborn. And slow. Eric wants to go to the park and play fetch, but Meatball likes to lie in the grass and drool. Is there anything Eric can do to get this bulldog to budge?

Oh No, Newf!

Yeti is a great dog.

Heidi is dog-crazy. So when she finds a friendly, abandoned Newfoundland, she's determined to take care of him. Even if her parents have forbidden her from bringing a dog home, she'll find a way—by keeping Yeti in her friend's shed!

There's just one thing . . .

Yeti is sweet, and Heidi wants to give him a real home. But he's also enormous and clumsy, and basically her parents' worst nightmare. Can Heidi turn him into a model dog? Or is Yeti just too big to handle?

Pet Trouble

Smarty-Pants
Sheltie

T. T. SUTHERLAND

SCHOLASTIC

Smarty-Pants Sheltie

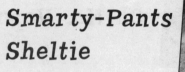

Jeopardy is a great dog.

Noah's family just moved, and Noah is nervous about starting a new school with new people. At least he can distract himself with the family's Shetland sheepdog, Jeopardy. Noah's mom suggests a dog agility class, which seems like an OK idea—at first.

There's just one thing . . .

Jeopardy is so embarrassing! When Noah takes her to class, she barks, runs away, and doesn't listen to him at all. Noah wants to make friends, not get laughed at chasing around this crazy dog! How will he ever fit in with this shouty Sheltie?